LEGO

LEGENDS OF CHIMA™

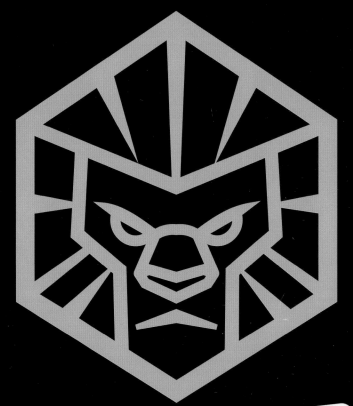

LEGO® LEGENDS OF CHIMA GRAPHIC NOVELS AVAILABLE FROM PAPERCUTZ™

LEGO
LEGENDS OF
CHIMA
ALL-NEW GRAPHIC NOVEL SERIES!
HIGH RISK!
YANNICK GROTHOLT
COMICON
PAPERCUTZ

#1 "High Risk!"

LEGO
LEGENDS OF
CHIMA
THE RIGHT DECISION
YANNICK GROTHOLT
COMICON
PAPERCUTZ

#2 "The Right Decision"

LEGO
LEGENDS OF
CHIMA
CHI QUEST!
YANNICK GROTHOLT
COMICON
PAPERCUTZ

#3 "CHI Quest!"

LEGO
LEGENDS OF
CHIMA
THE POWER OF FIRE CHI
YANNICK GROTHOLT
COMICON
PAPERCUTZ

#4 "The Power of Fire Chi"

LEGO
LEGENDS OF
CHIMA
WINGS FOR A LION
YANNICK GROTHOLT
COMICON
PAPERCUTZ

#5 "Wings for a Lion"

LEGO
LEGENDS OF
CHIMA
PLAYING WITH FIRE
YANNICK GROTHOLT
COMICON
PAPERCUTZ

#6 "Playing With Fire!"

LEGO LEGENDS OF CHIMA graphic novels are available for $7.99 in paperback, $12.99 in hardcover.
Available from booksellers everywhere. You can also order online from Papercutz.com.
Or call 1-800-886-1223, Monday through Friday, 9-5 EST. MC, Visa, and AmEx accepted.
To order by mail, please add $4.00 for postage and handling for first book ordered,
$1.00 for each additional book and make check payable to NBM Publishing.
Send to: Papercutz, 160 Broadway, Suite 700, East Wing, New York, NY 10038.

LEGO LEGENDS OF CHIMA graphic novels are also available digitally wherever e-books are sold.

Papercutz.com

FSC
www.fsc.org
MIX
Paper from responsible sources
FSC® C006398

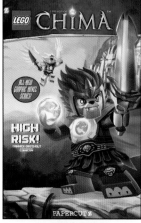

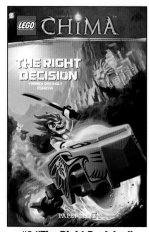

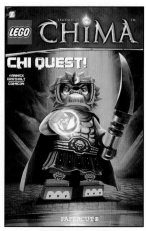

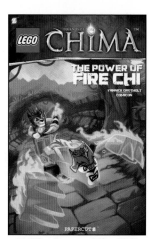

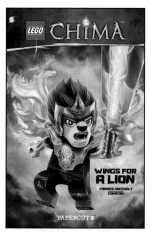

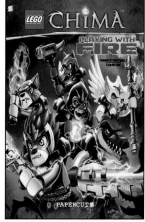

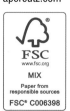

Yannick Grotholt
Writer

Comicon
Artist

New York

LEGO ® LEGENDS OF CHIMA
#6 "Playing With Fire"
Yannick Grotholt – Writer
Comicon (Pencils: Miguel Sanchez, Inks: Marc Alberich, Color: Oriol San Julian) – Artist
Tom Orzechowski – Letterer
Asante Simons, Emily Wixted – Editorial Interns
Jeff Whitman – Production Coordinator
Bethany Bryan – Associate Editor
Jim Salicrup
Editor-in-Chief

ISBN: 978-1-62991-457-2 paperback edition
ISBN: 978-1-62991-458-9 hardcover edition

Printed in Hong Kong
January 2016 by Asia One Printing LTD
13/F Asia One Tower
8 Fung Yip St., Chaiwan
Hong Kong

Papercutz books may be purchased for business or promotional use.
For information on bulk purchases please contact Macmillan Corporate
and Premium Sales Department at (800) 221-7945 x5442.

Distributed by Macmillan
First Papercutz Printing

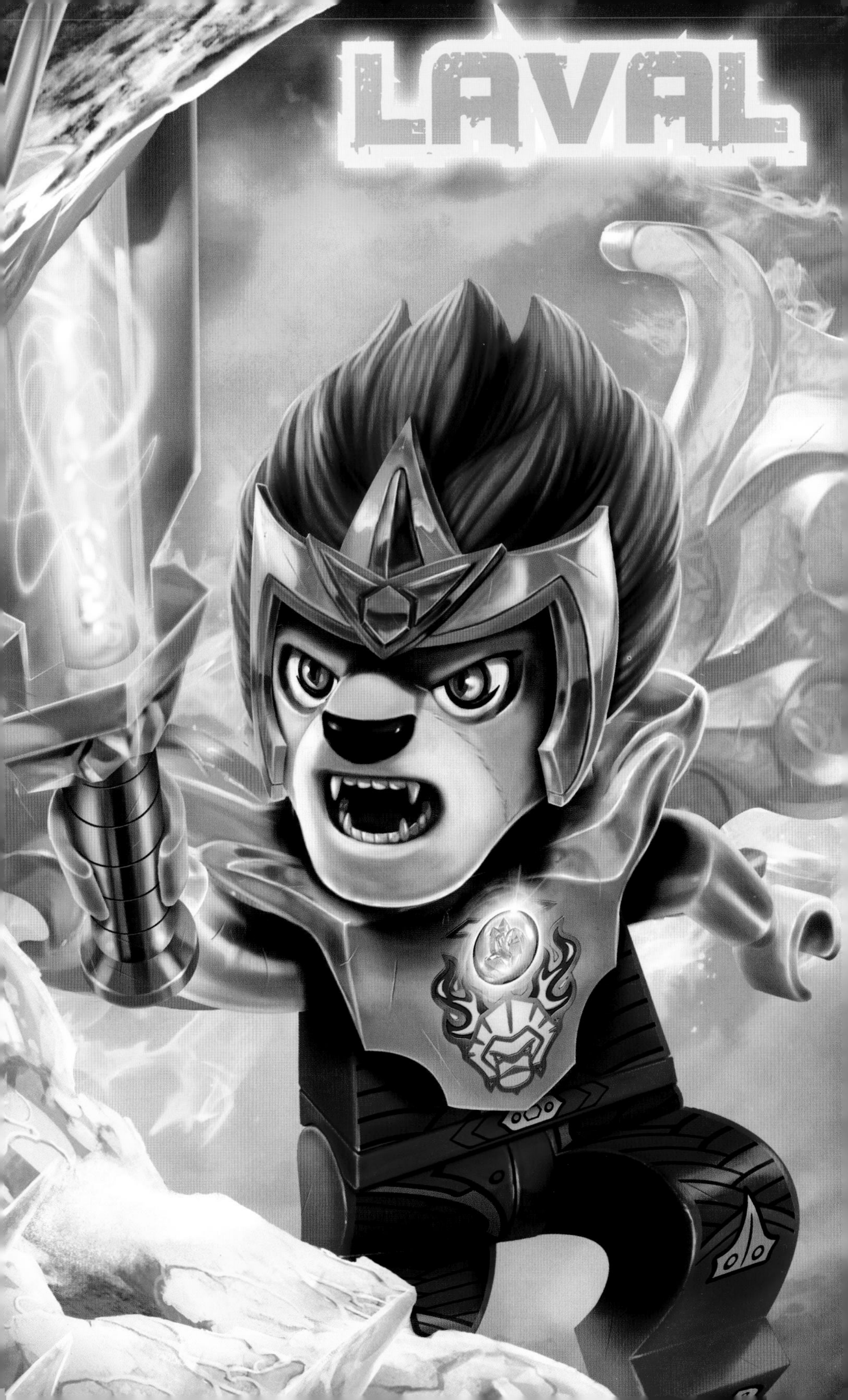
LAVAL

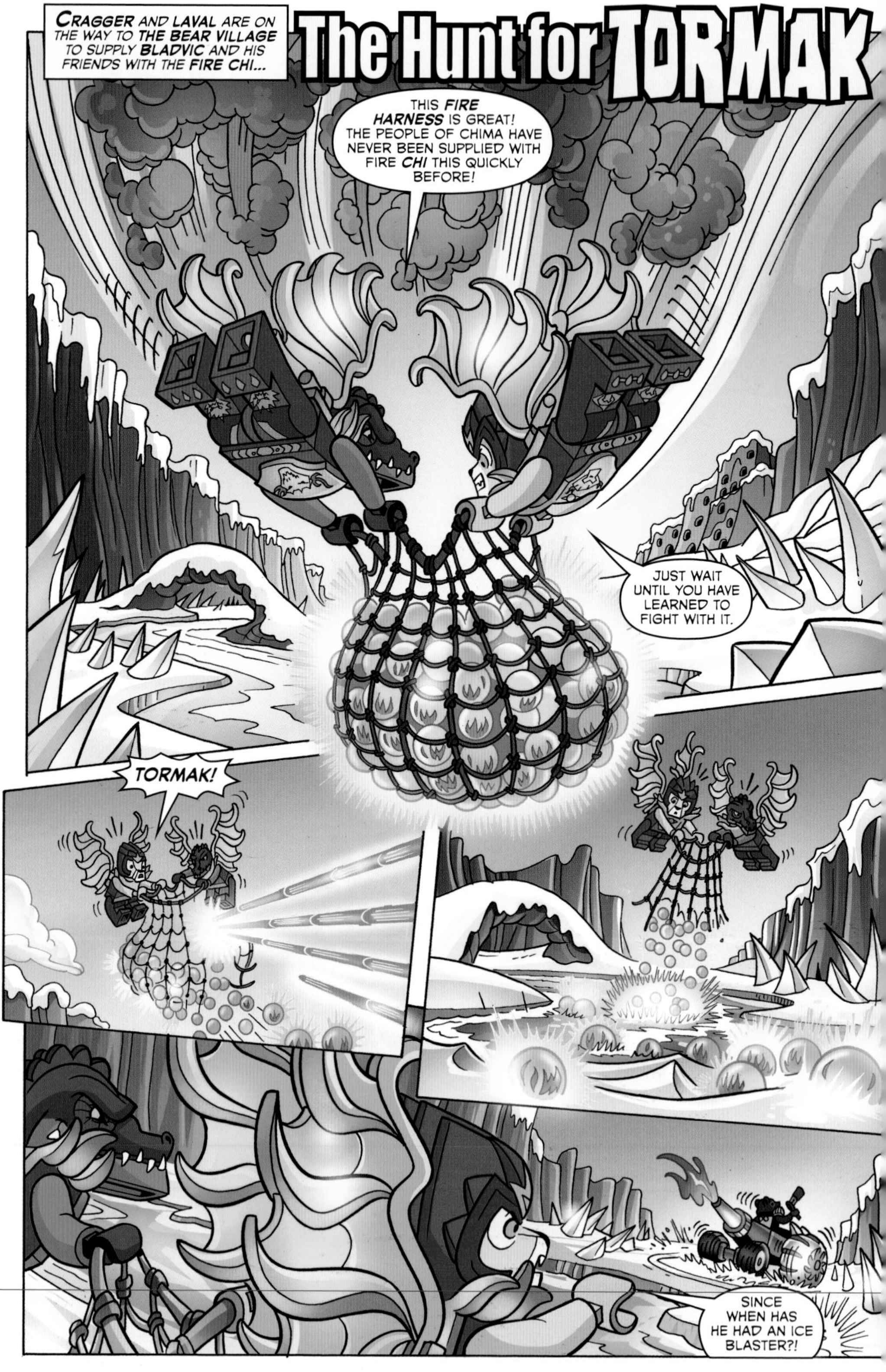
CRAGGER AND LAVAL ARE ON THE WAY TO THE BEAR VILLAGE TO SUPPLY BLADVIC AND HIS FRIENDS WITH THE FIRE CHI...
The Hunt for TORMAK
THIS FIRE HARNESS IS GREAT! THE PEOPLE OF CHIMA HAVE NEVER BEEN SUPPLIED WITH FIRE CHI THIS QUICKLY BEFORE!
JUST WAIT UNTIL YOU HAVE LEARNED TO FIGHT WITH IT.
TORMAK!
SINCE WHEN HAS HE HAD AN ICE BLASTER?!

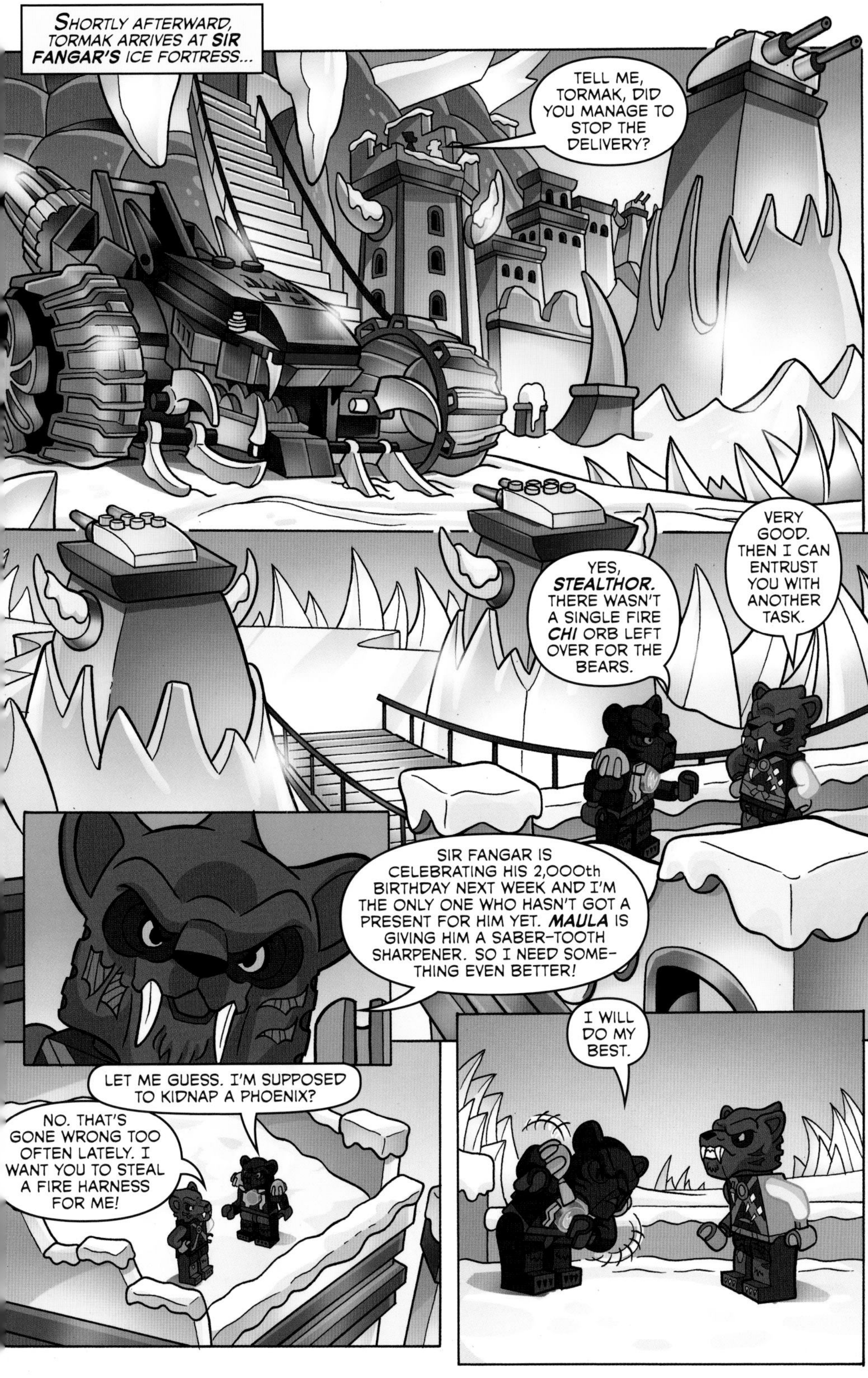
SHORTLY AFTERWARD, TORMAK ARRIVES AT SIR FANGAR'S ICE FORTRESS...
TELL ME, TORMAK, DID YOU MANAGE TO STOP THE DELIVERY?
YES, STEALTHOR. THERE WASN'T A SINGLE FIRE CHI ORB LEFT OVER FOR THE BEARS.
VERY GOOD. THEN I CAN ENTRUST YOU WITH ANOTHER TASK.
SIR FANGAR IS CELEBRATING HIS 2,000th BIRTHDAY NEXT WEEK AND I'M THE ONLY ONE WHO HASN'T GOT A PRESENT FOR HIM YET. MAULA IS GIVING HIM A SABER-TOOTH SHARPENER. SO I NEED SOMETHING EVEN BETTER!
I WILL DO MY BEST.
LET ME GUESS. I'M SUPPOSED TO KIDNAP A PHOENIX?
NO. THAT'S GONE WRONG TOO OFTEN LATELY. I WANT YOU TO STEAL A FIRE HARNESS FOR ME!

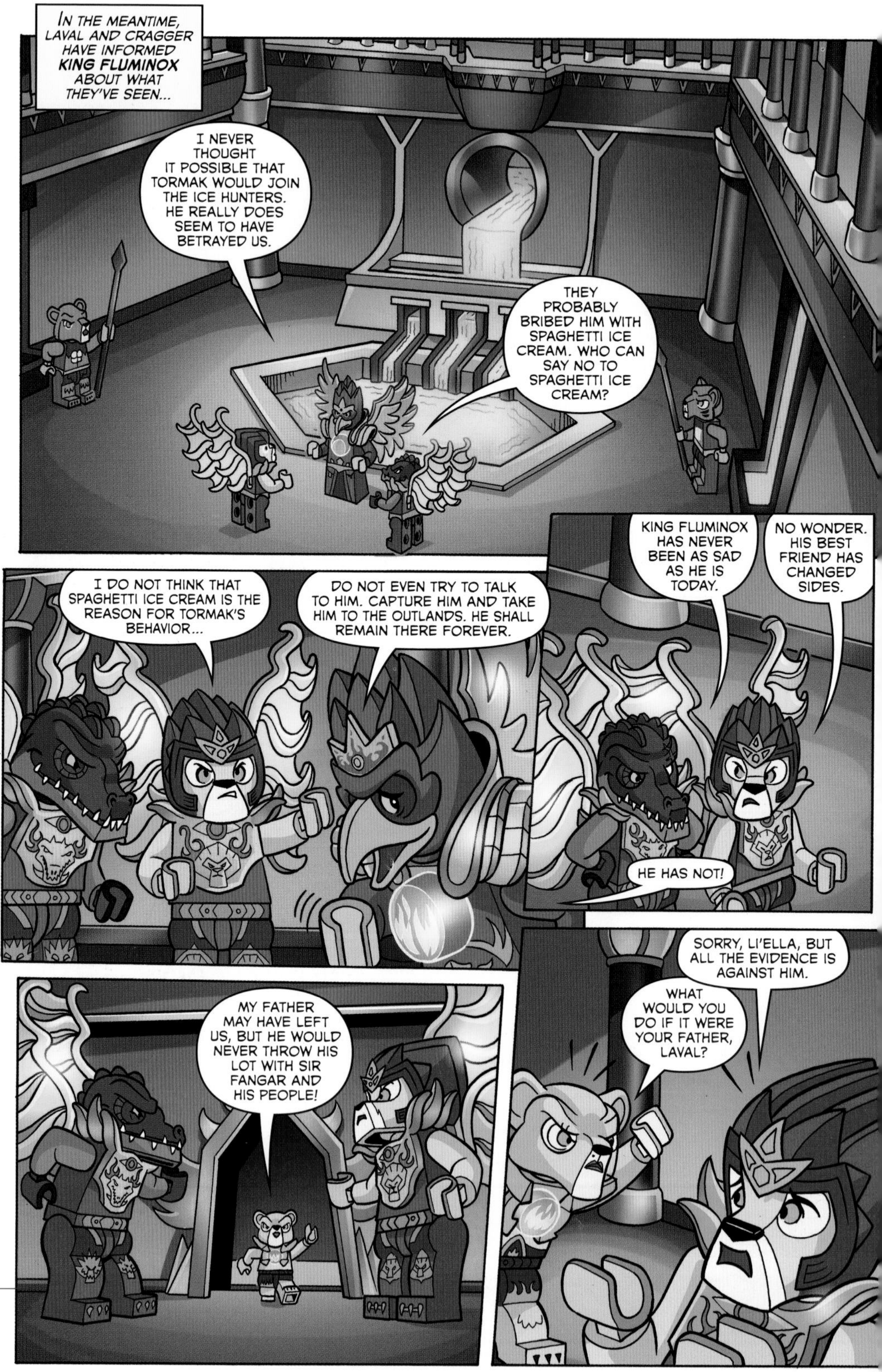

IN THE MEANTIME, LAVAL AND CRAGGER HAVE INFORMED KING FLUMINOX ABOUT WHAT THEY'VE SEEN...
I NEVER THOUGHT IT POSSIBLE THAT TORMAK WOULD JOIN THE ICE HUNTERS. HE REALLY DOES SEEM TO HAVE BETRAYED US.
THEY PROBABLY BRIBED HIM WITH SPAGHETTI ICE CREAM. WHO CAN SAY NO TO SPAGHETTI ICE CREAM?
I DO NOT THINK THAT SPAGHETTI ICE CREAM IS THE REASON FOR TORMAK'S BEHAVIOR...
DO NOT EVEN TRY TO TALK TO HIM. CAPTURE HIM AND TAKE HIM TO THE OUTLANDS. HE SHALL REMAIN THERE FOREVER.
KING FLUMINOX HAS NEVER BEEN AS SAD AS HE IS TODAY.
NO WONDER. HIS BEST FRIEND HAS CHANGED SIDES.
HE HAS NOT!
MY FATHER MAY HAVE LEFT US, BUT HE WOULD NEVER THROW HIS LOT WITH SIR FANGAR AND HIS PEOPLE!
SORRY, LI'ELLA, BUT ALL THE EVIDENCE IS AGAINST HIM.
WHAT WOULD YOU DO IF IT WERE YOUR FATHER, LAVAL?

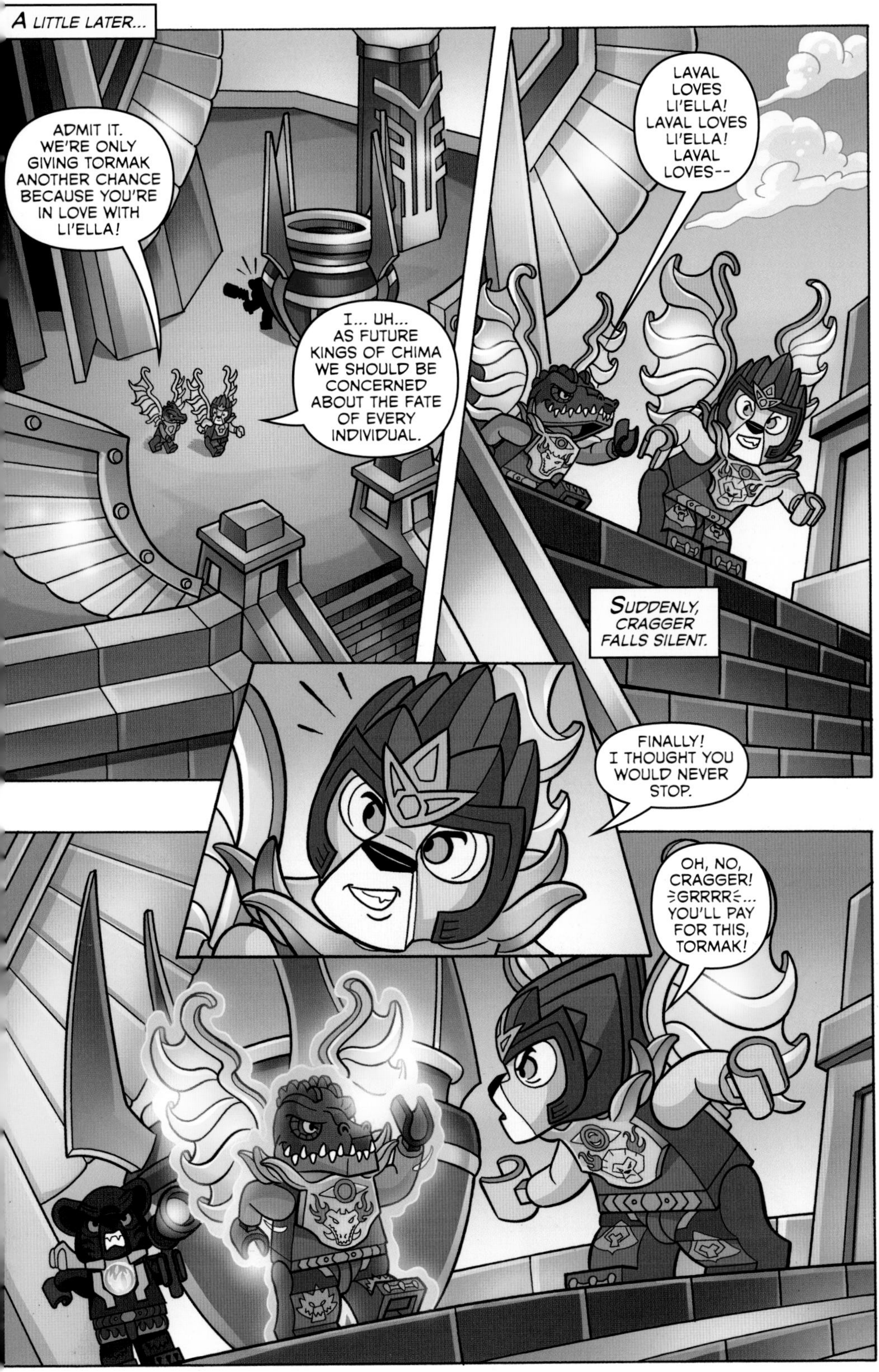
A LITTLE LATER...
ADMIT IT. WE'RE ONLY GIVING TORMAK ANOTHER CHANCE BECAUSE YOU'RE IN LOVE WITH LI'ELLA!
I... UH... AS FUTURE KINGS OF CHIMA WE SHOULD BE CONCERNED ABOUT THE FATE OF EVERY INDIVIDUAL.
LAVAL LOVES LI'ELLA! LAVAL LOVES LI'ELLA! LAVAL LOVES--
SUDDENLY, CRAGGER FALLS SILENT.
FINALLY! I THOUGHT YOU WOULD NEVER STOP.
OH, NO, CRAGGER! GRRRR... YOU'LL PAY FOR THIS, TORMAK!

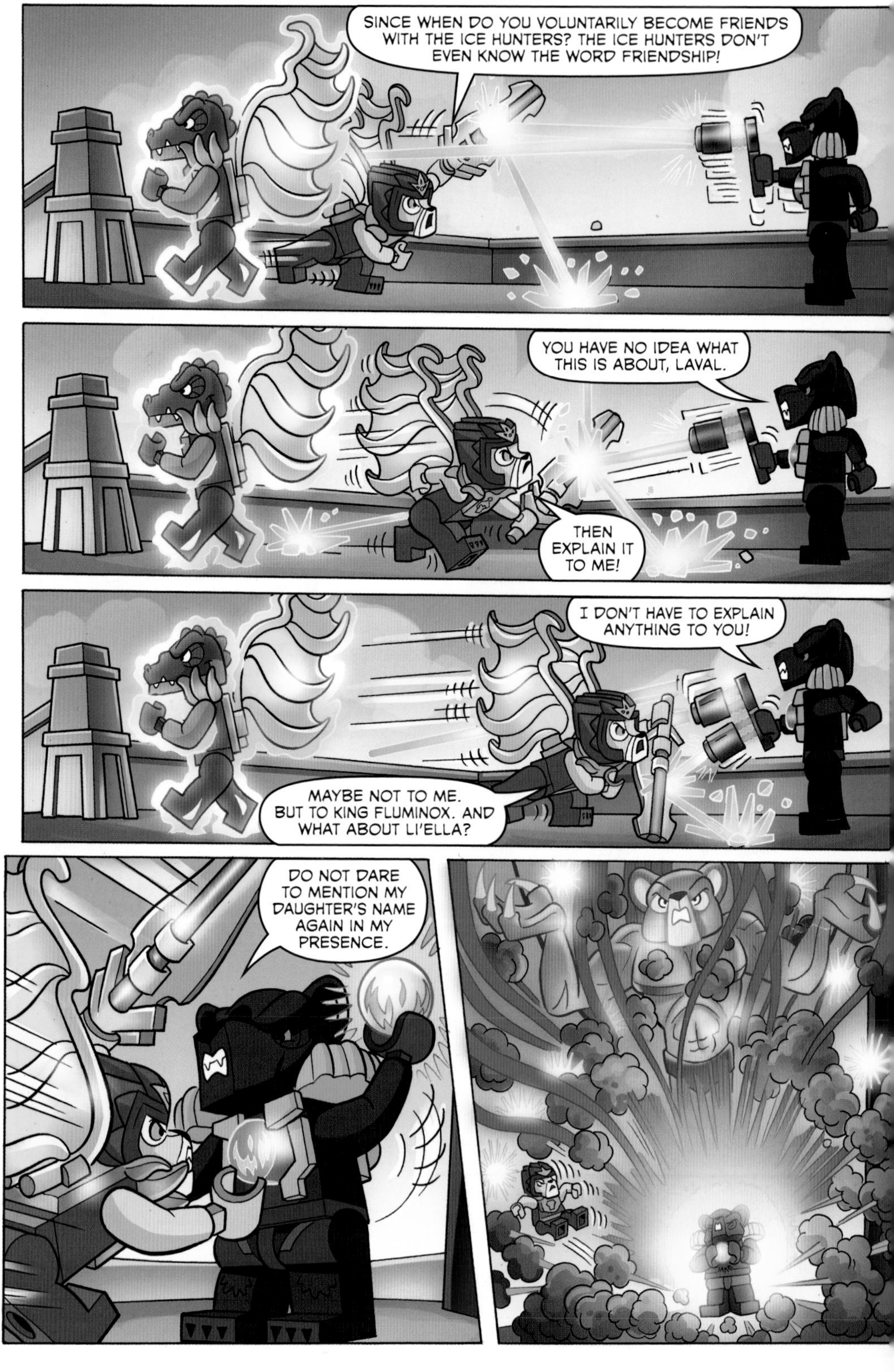
SINCE WHEN DO YOU VOLUNTARILY BECOME FRIENDS WITH THE ICE HUNTERS? THE ICE HUNTERS DON'T EVEN KNOW THE WORD FRIENDSHIP!
YOU HAVE NO IDEA WHAT THIS IS ABOUT, LAVAL.
THEN EXPLAIN IT TO ME!
I DON'T HAVE TO EXPLAIN ANYTHING TO YOU!
MAYBE NOT TO ME. BUT TO KING FLUMINOX. AND WHAT ABOUT LI'ELLA?
DO NOT DARE TO MENTION MY DAUGHTER'S NAME AGAIN IN MY PRESENCE.

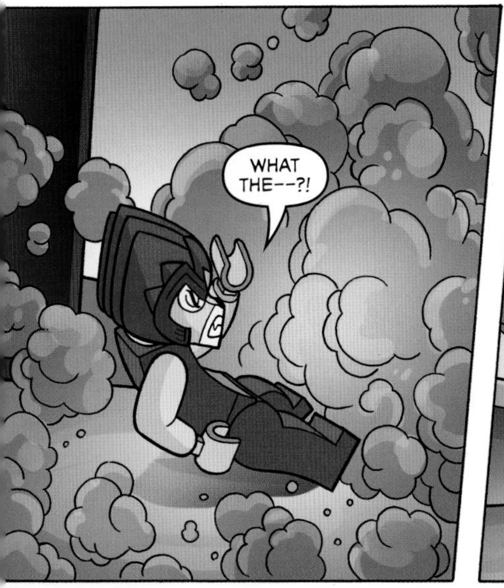
WHAT THE--?!
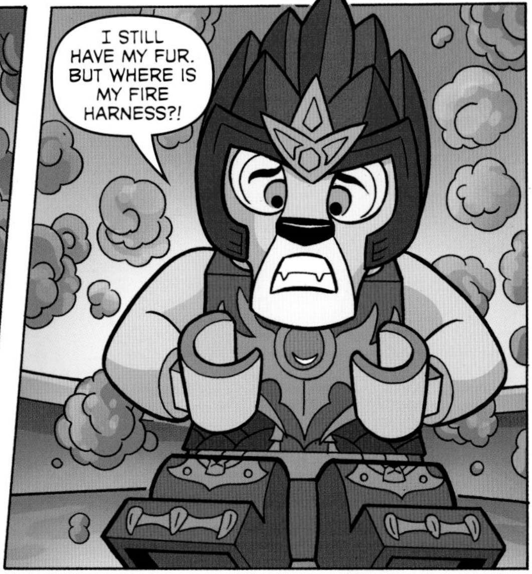
I STILL HAVE MY FUR. BUT WHERE IS MY FIRE HARNESS?!
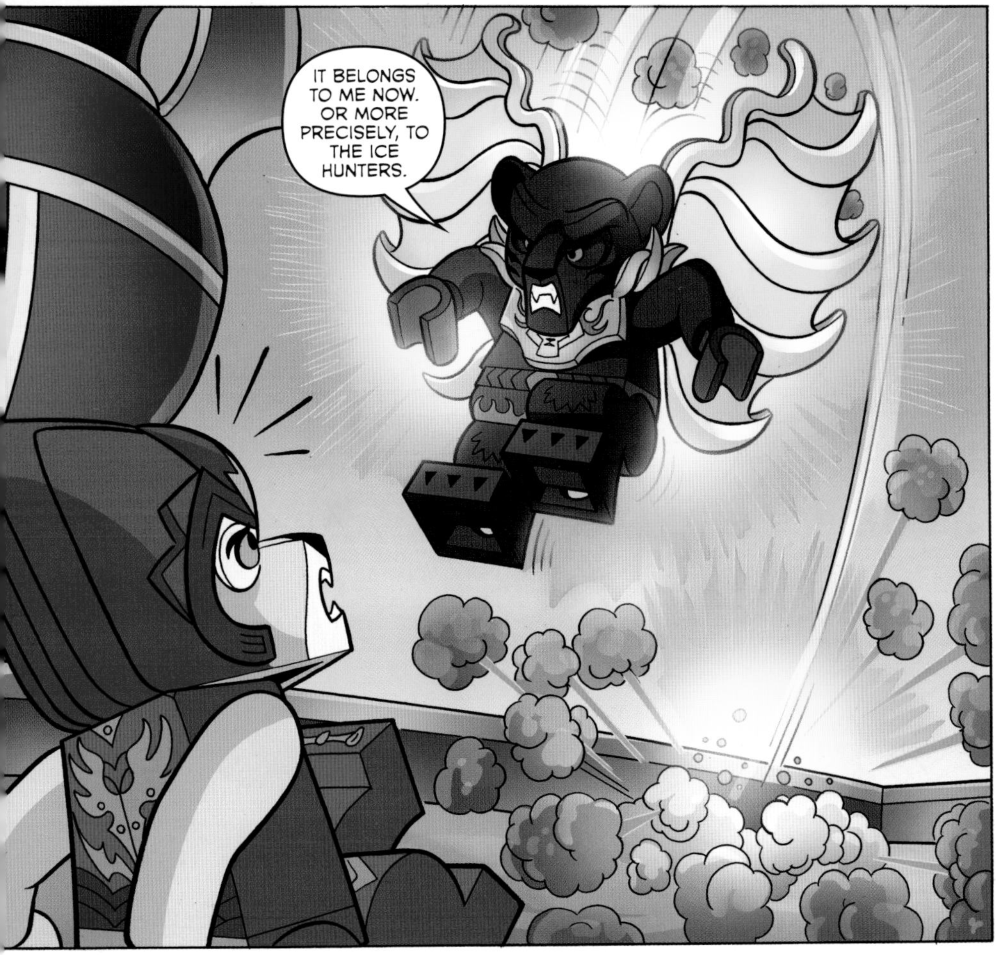
IT BELONGS TO ME NOW. OR MORE PRECISELY, TO THE ICE HUNTERS.

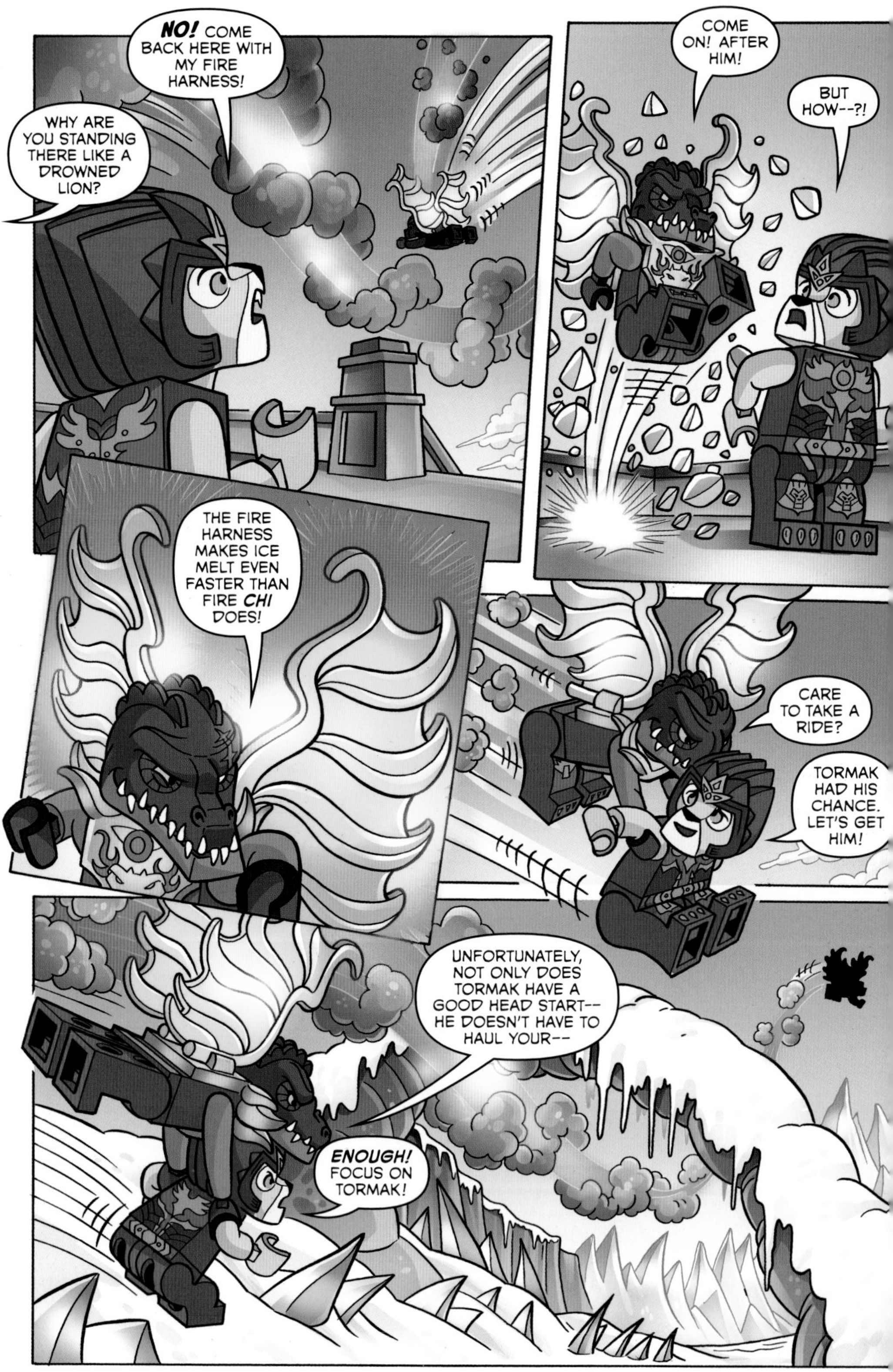
NO! COME BACK HERE WITH MY FIRE HARNESS!
WHY ARE YOU STANDING THERE LIKE A DROWNED LION?
COME ON! AFTER HIM!
BUT HOW--?!
THE FIRE HARNESS MAKES ICE MELT EVEN FASTER THAN FIRE CHI DOES!
CARE TO TAKE A RIDE?
TORMAK HAD HIS CHANCE. LET'S GET HIM!
UNFORTUNATELY, NOT ONLY DOES TORMAK HAVE A GOOD HEAD START-- HE DOESN'T HAVE TO HAUL YOUR--
ENOUGH! FOCUS ON TORMAK!

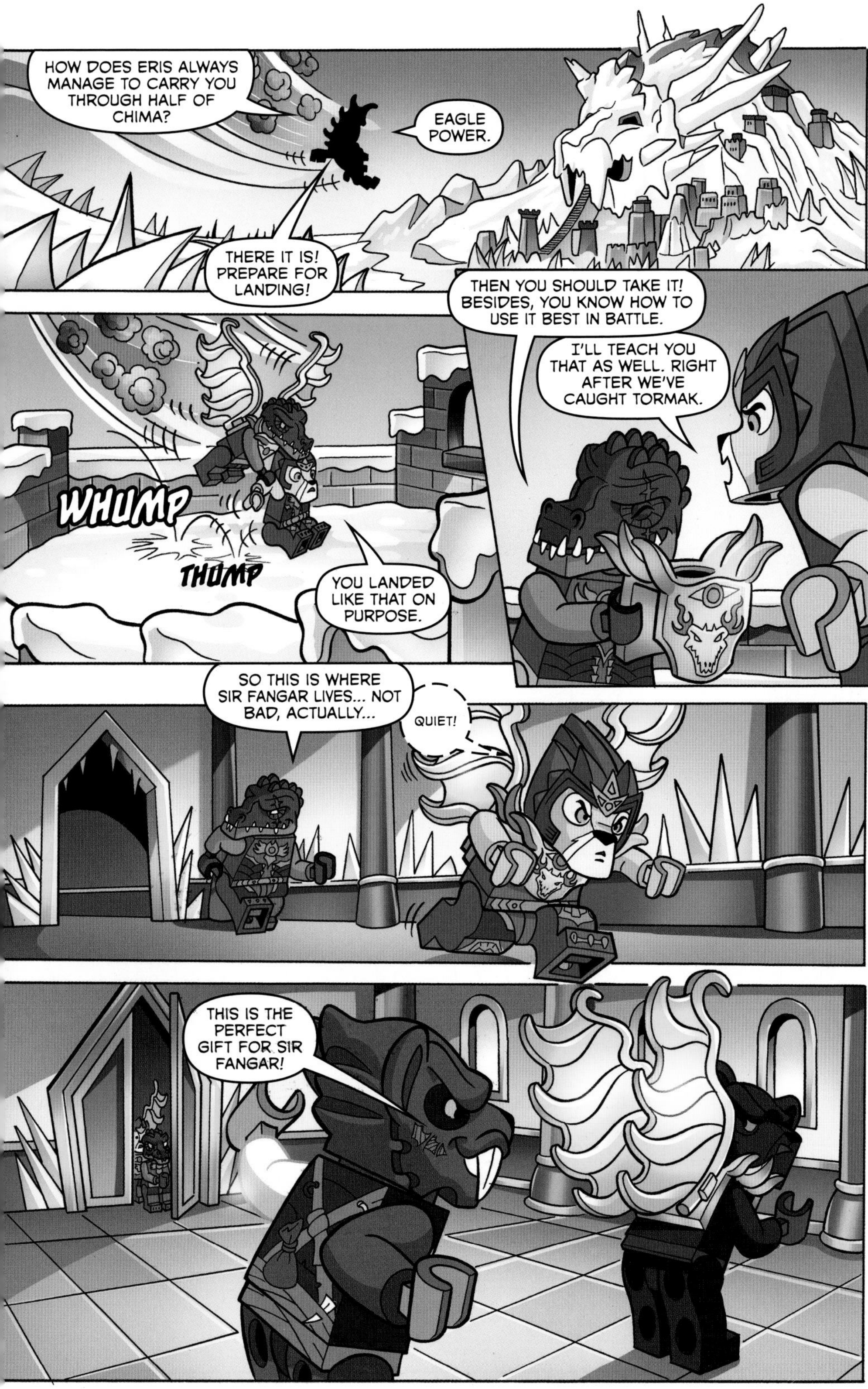
HOW DOES ERIS ALWAYS MANAGE TO CARRY YOU THROUGH HALF OF CHIMA?
EAGLE POWER.
THERE IT IS! PREPARE FOR LANDING!
WHUMP
THUMP
YOU LANDED LIKE THAT ON PURPOSE.
THEN YOU SHOULD TAKE IT! BESIDES, YOU KNOW HOW TO USE IT BEST IN BATTLE.
I'LL TEACH YOU THAT AS WELL. RIGHT AFTER WE'VE CAUGHT TORMAK.
SO THIS IS WHERE SIR FANGAR LIVES... NOT BAD, ACTUALLY...
QUIET!
THIS IS THE PERFECT GIFT FOR SIR FANGAR!

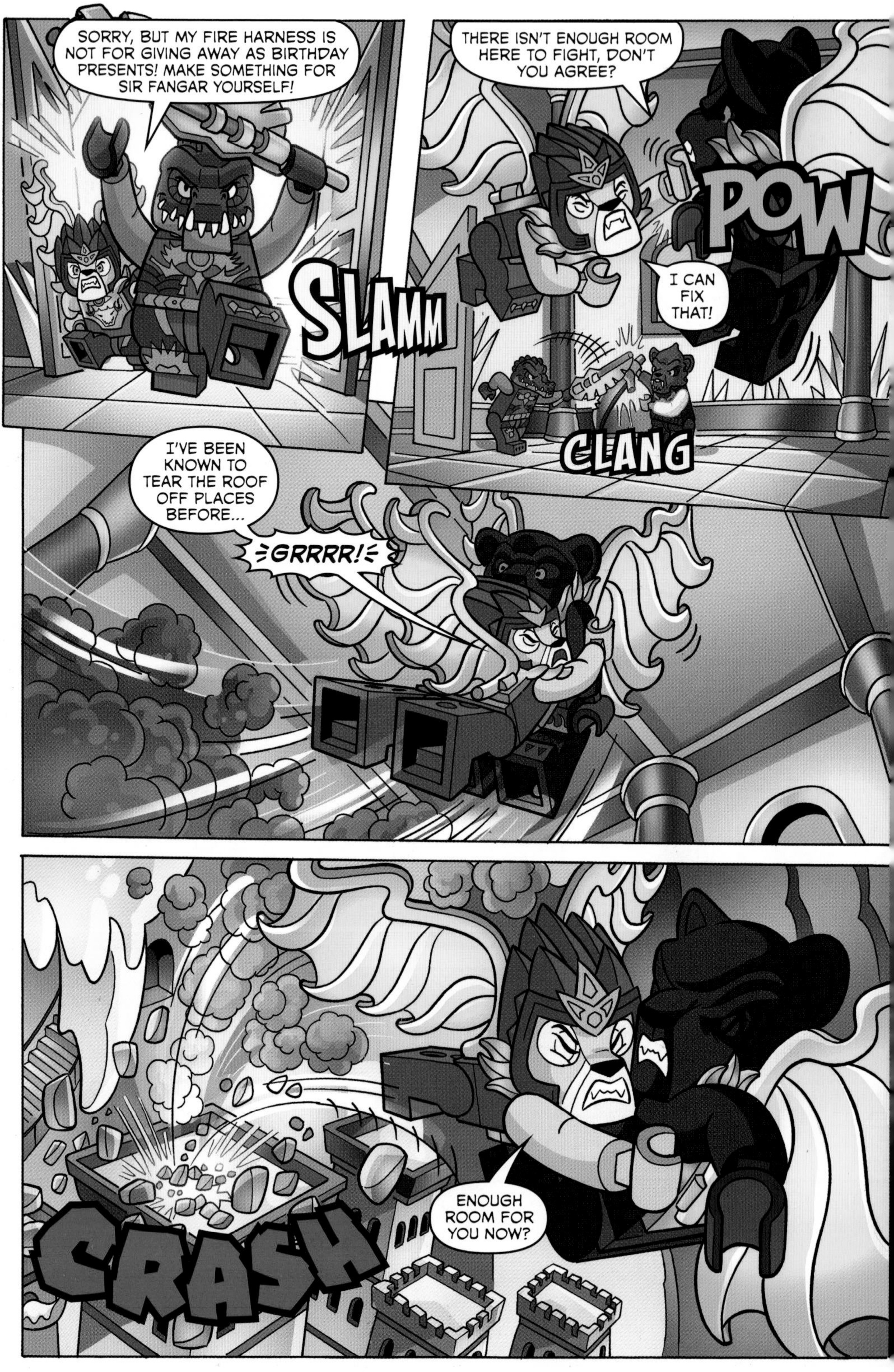
SORRY, BUT MY FIRE HARNESS IS NOT FOR GIVING AWAY AS BIRTHDAY PRESENTS! MAKE SOMETHING FOR SIR FANGAR YOURSELF!
SLAMM
THERE ISN'T ENOUGH ROOM HERE TO FIGHT, DON'T YOU AGREE?
POW
I CAN FIX THAT!
CLANG
I'VE BEEN KNOWN TO TEAR THE ROOF OFF PLACES BEFORE...
GRRRR!
ENOUGH ROOM FOR YOU NOW?
CRASH

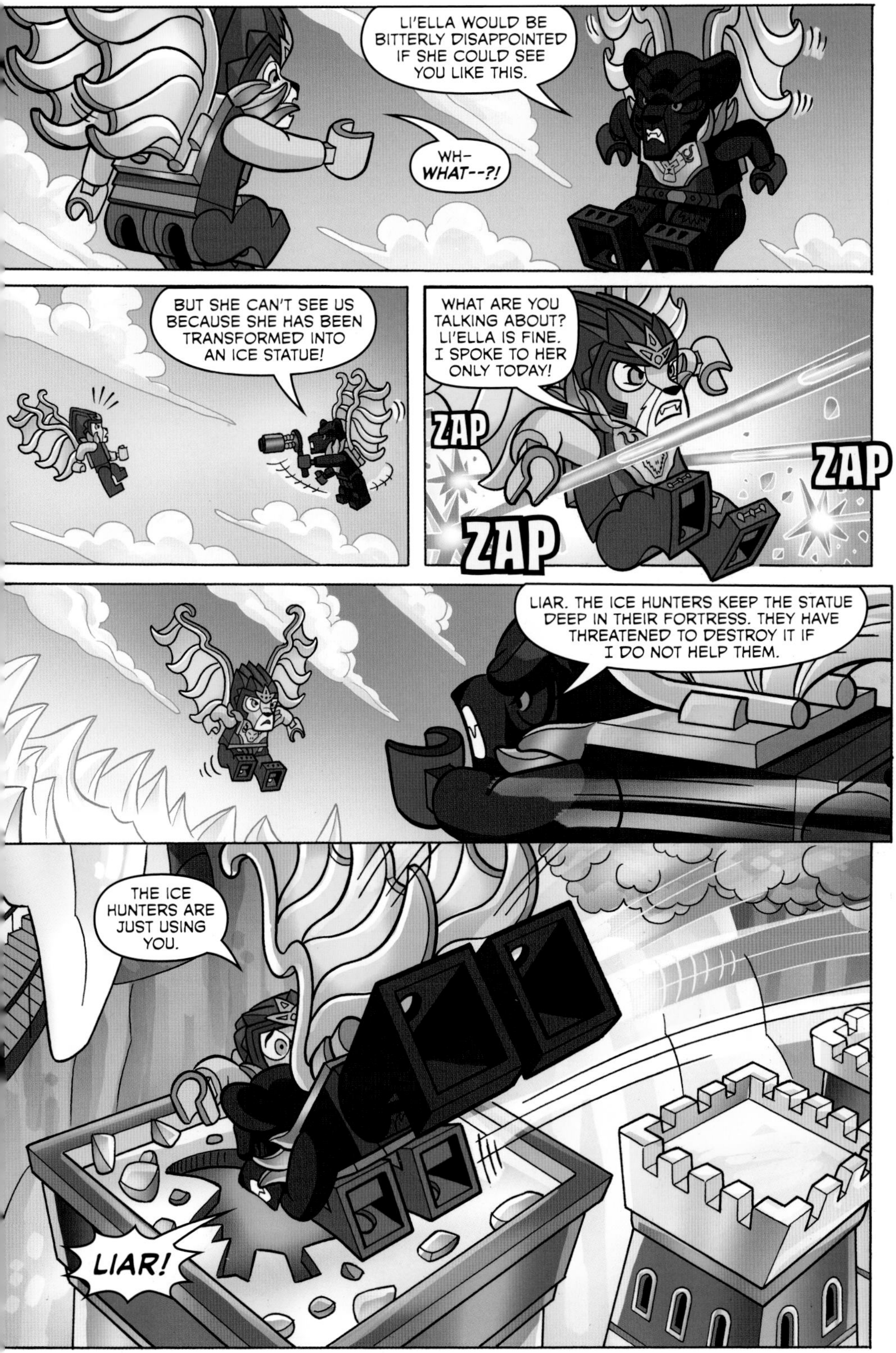
LI'ELLA WOULD BE BITTERLY DISAPPOINTED IF SHE COULD SEE YOU LIKE THIS.
WH- WHAT--?!
BUT SHE CAN'T SEE US BECAUSE SHE HAS BEEN TRANSFORMED INTO AN ICE STATUE!
WHAT ARE YOU TALKING ABOUT? LI'ELLA IS FINE. I SPOKE TO HER ONLY TODAY!
ZAP
ZAP
ZAP
LIAR. THE ICE HUNTERS KEEP THE STATUE DEEP IN THEIR FORTRESS. THEY HAVE THREATENED TO DESTROY IT IF I DO NOT HELP THEM.
THE ICE HUNTERS ARE JUST USING YOU.
LIAR!

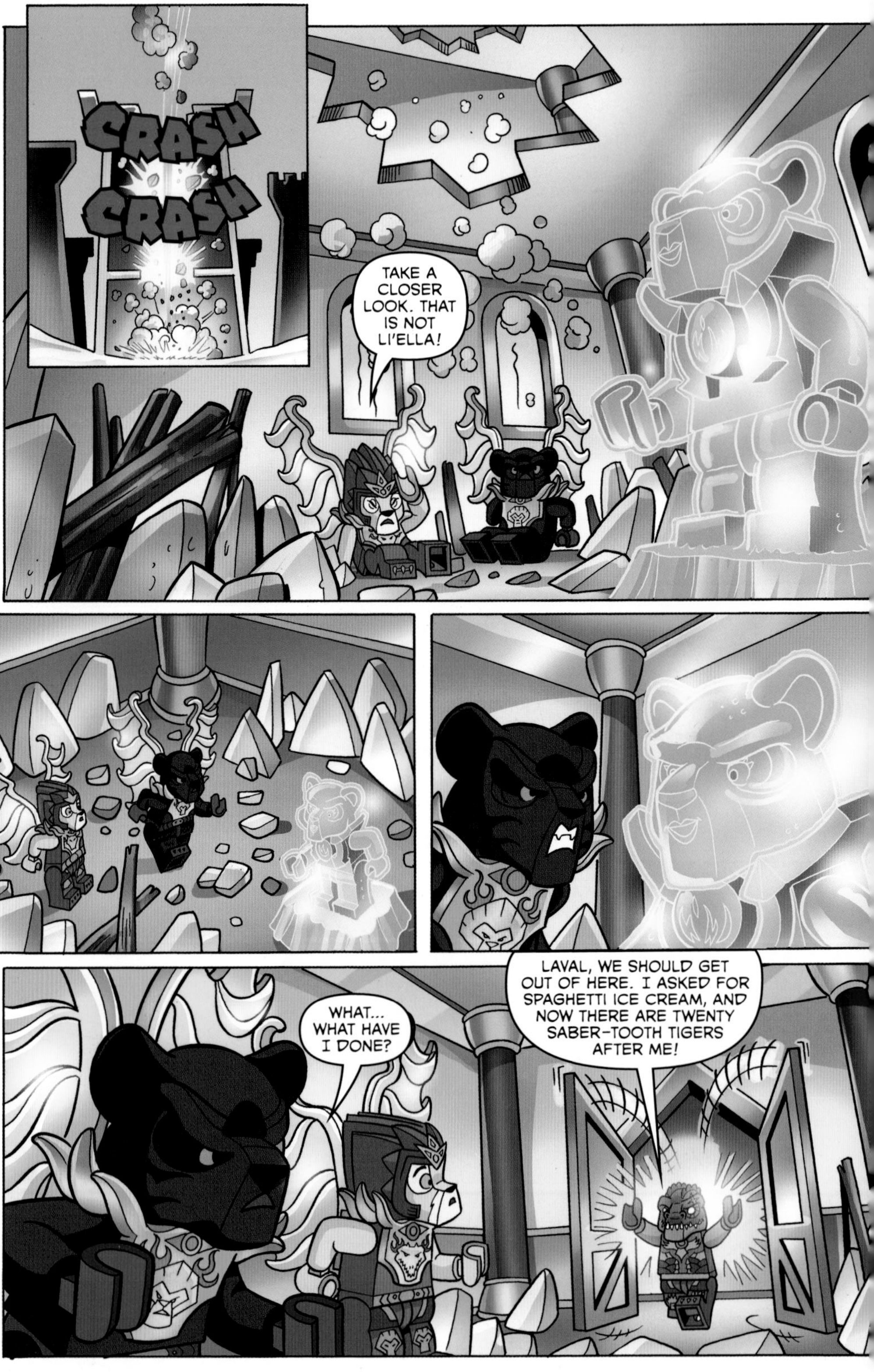
CRASH
CRASH
TAKE A CLOSER LOOK. THAT IS NOT LI'ELLA!
WHAT... WHAT HAVE I DONE?
LAVAL, WE SHOULD GET OUT OF HERE. I ASKED FOR SPAGHETTI ICE CREAM, AND NOW THERE ARE TWENTY SABER-TOOTH TIGERS AFTER ME!

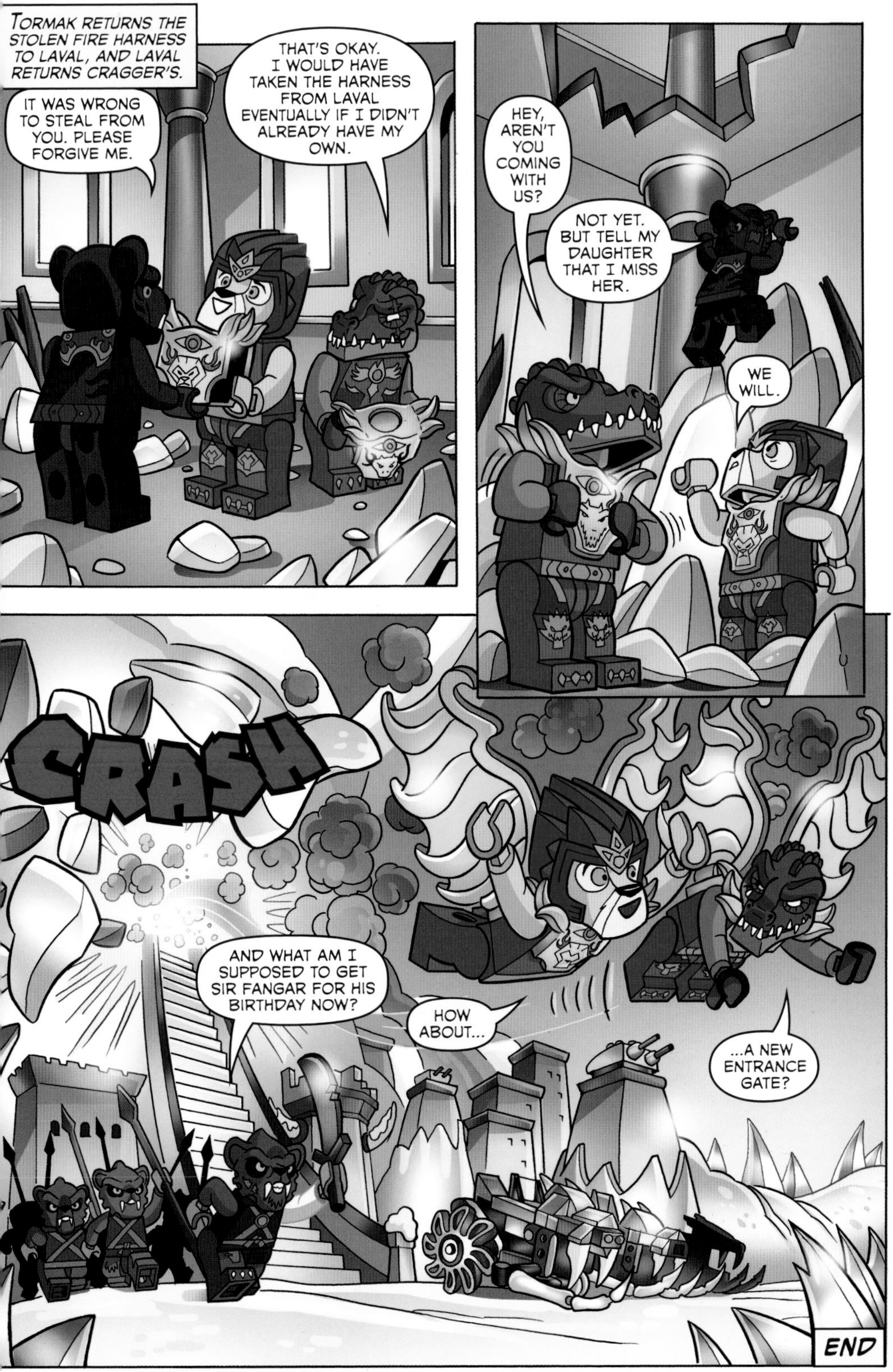
TORMAK RETURNS THE STOLEN FIRE HARNESS TO LAVAL, AND LAVAL RETURNS CRAGGER'S.
IT WAS WRONG TO STEAL FROM YOU. PLEASE FORGIVE ME.
THAT'S OKAY. I WOULD HAVE TAKEN THE HARNESS FROM LAVAL EVENTUALLY IF I DIDN'T ALREADY HAVE MY OWN.
HEY, AREN'T YOU COMING WITH US?
NOT YET. BUT TELL MY DAUGHTER THAT I MISS HER.
WE WILL.
CRASH
AND WHAT AM I SUPPOSED TO GET SIR FANGAR FOR HIS BIRTHDAY NOW?
HOW ABOUT...
...A NEW ENTRANCE GATE?
END

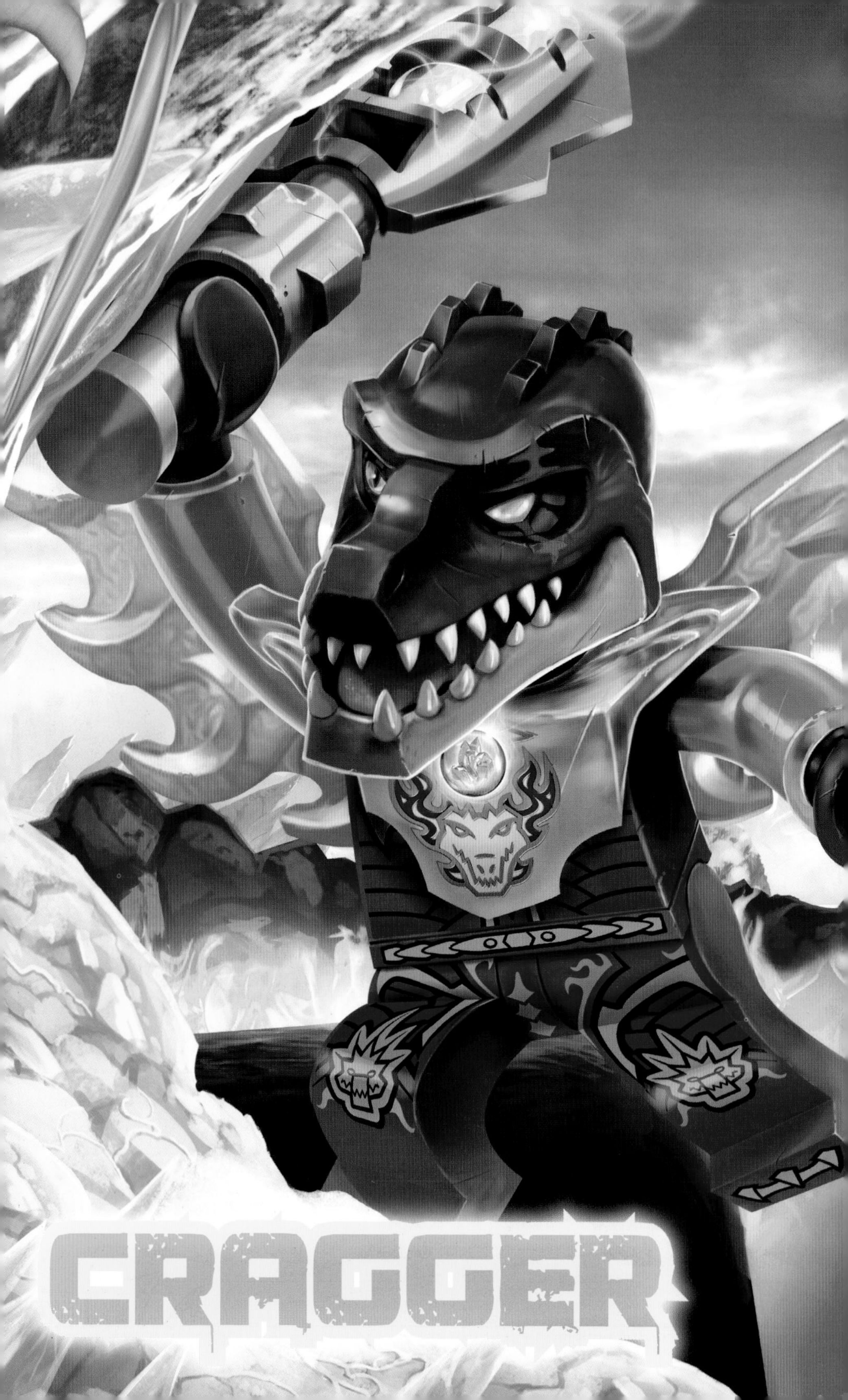
CRAGGER

The Great Illumination

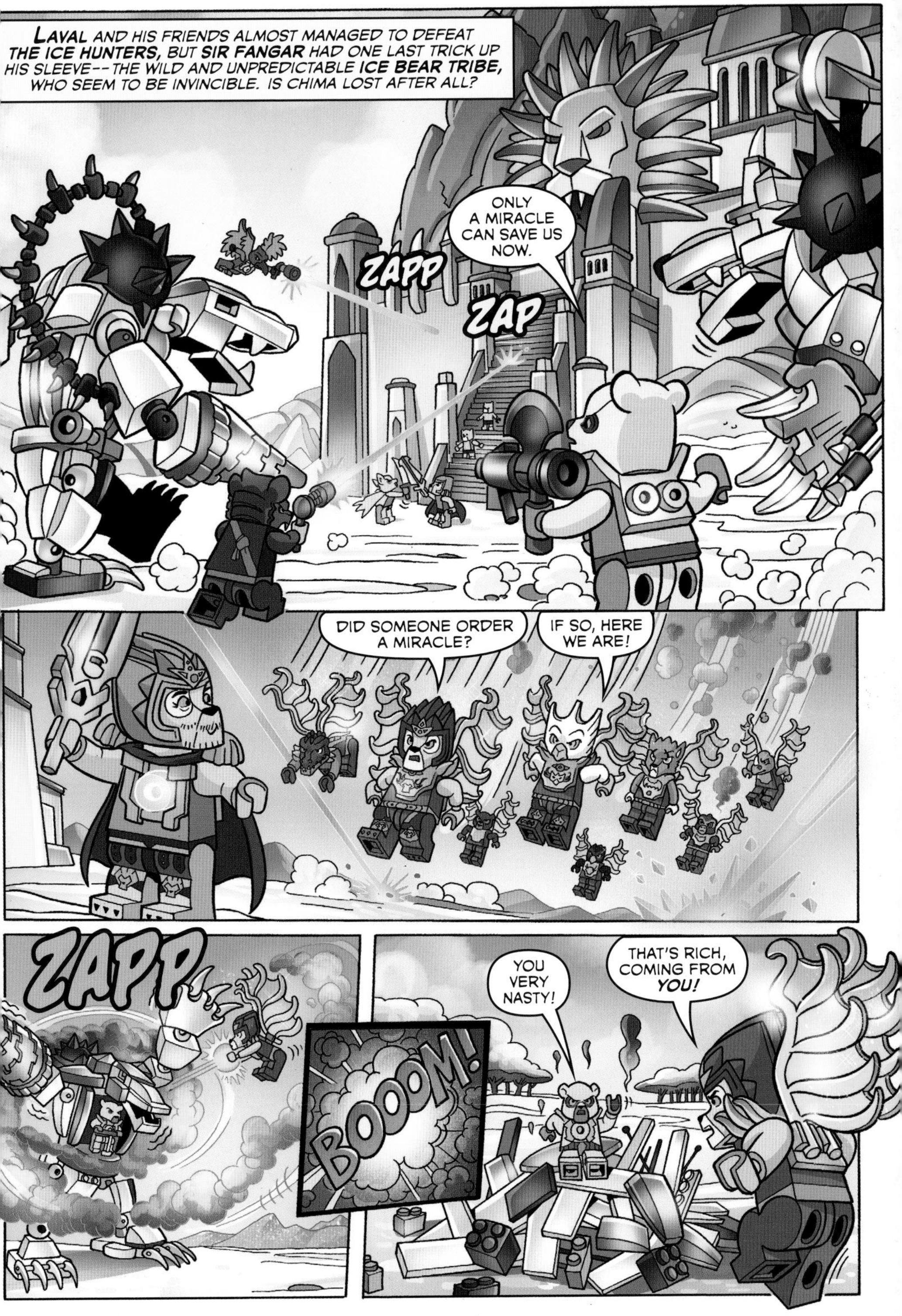

LAVAL AND HIS FRIENDS ALMOST MANAGED TO DEFEAT THE ICE HUNTERS, BUT SIR FANGAR HAD ONE LAST TRICK UP HIS SLEEVE--THE WILD AND UNPREDICTABLE ICE BEAR TRIBE, WHO SEEM TO BE INVINCIBLE. IS CHIMA LOST AFTER ALL?
ONLY A MIRACLE CAN SAVE US NOW.
ZAPP
ZAP
DID SOMEONE ORDER A MIRACLE?
IF SO, HERE WE ARE!
ZAPP
BOOOM!
YOU VERY NASTY!
THAT'S RICH, COMING FROM *YOU!*

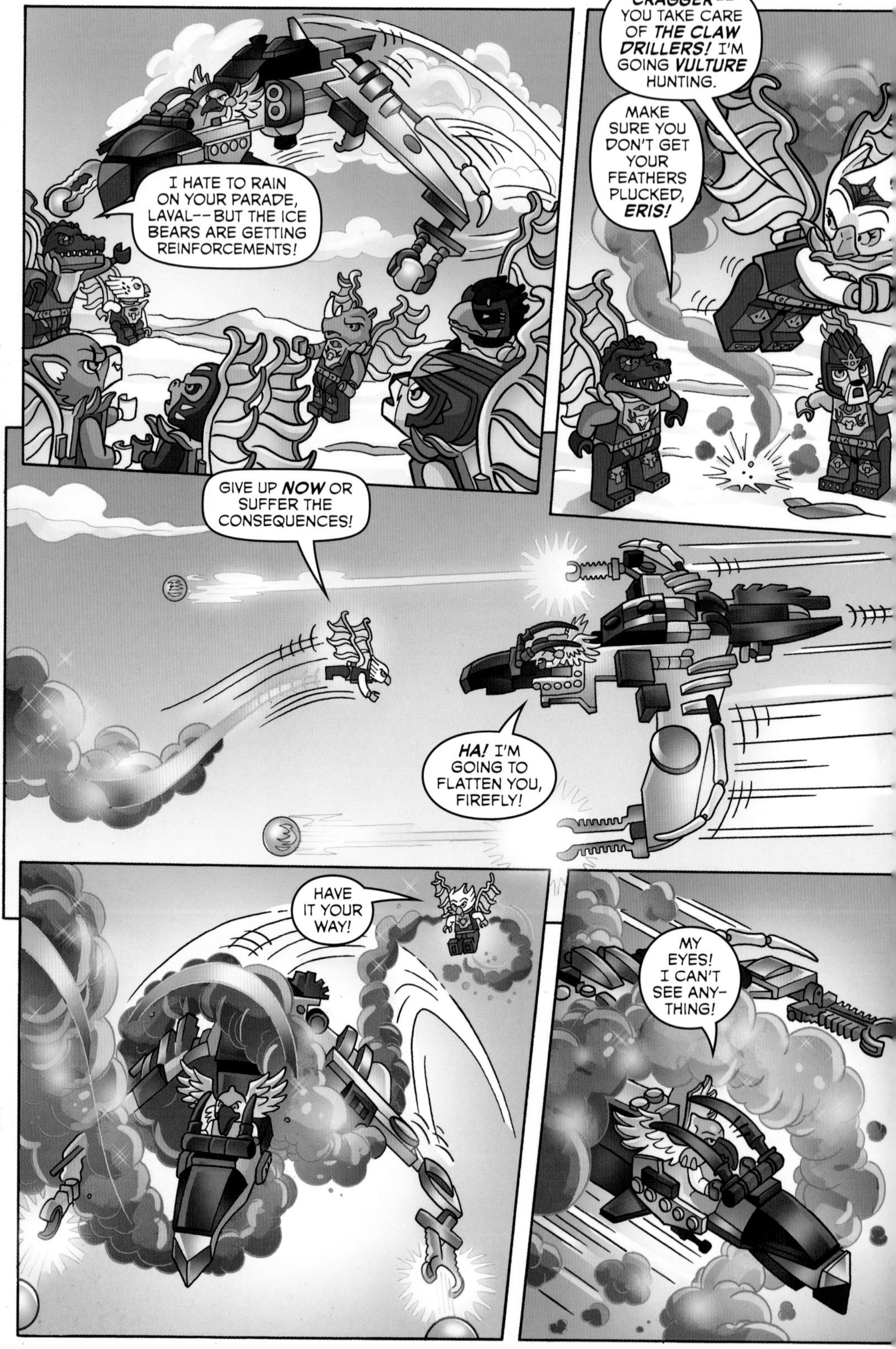
I HATE TO RAIN ON YOUR PARADE, LAVAL--BUT THE ICE BEARS ARE GETTING REINFORCEMENTS!
CRAGGER-- YOU TAKE CARE OF THE CLAW DRILLERS! I'M GOING VULTURE HUNTING.
MAKE SURE YOU DON'T GET YOUR FEATHERS PLUCKED, ERIS!
GIVE UP NOW OR SUFFER THE CONSEQUENCES!
HA! I'M GOING TO FLATTEN YOU, FIREFLY!
HAVE IT YOUR WAY!
MY EYES! I CAN'T SEE ANY-THING!

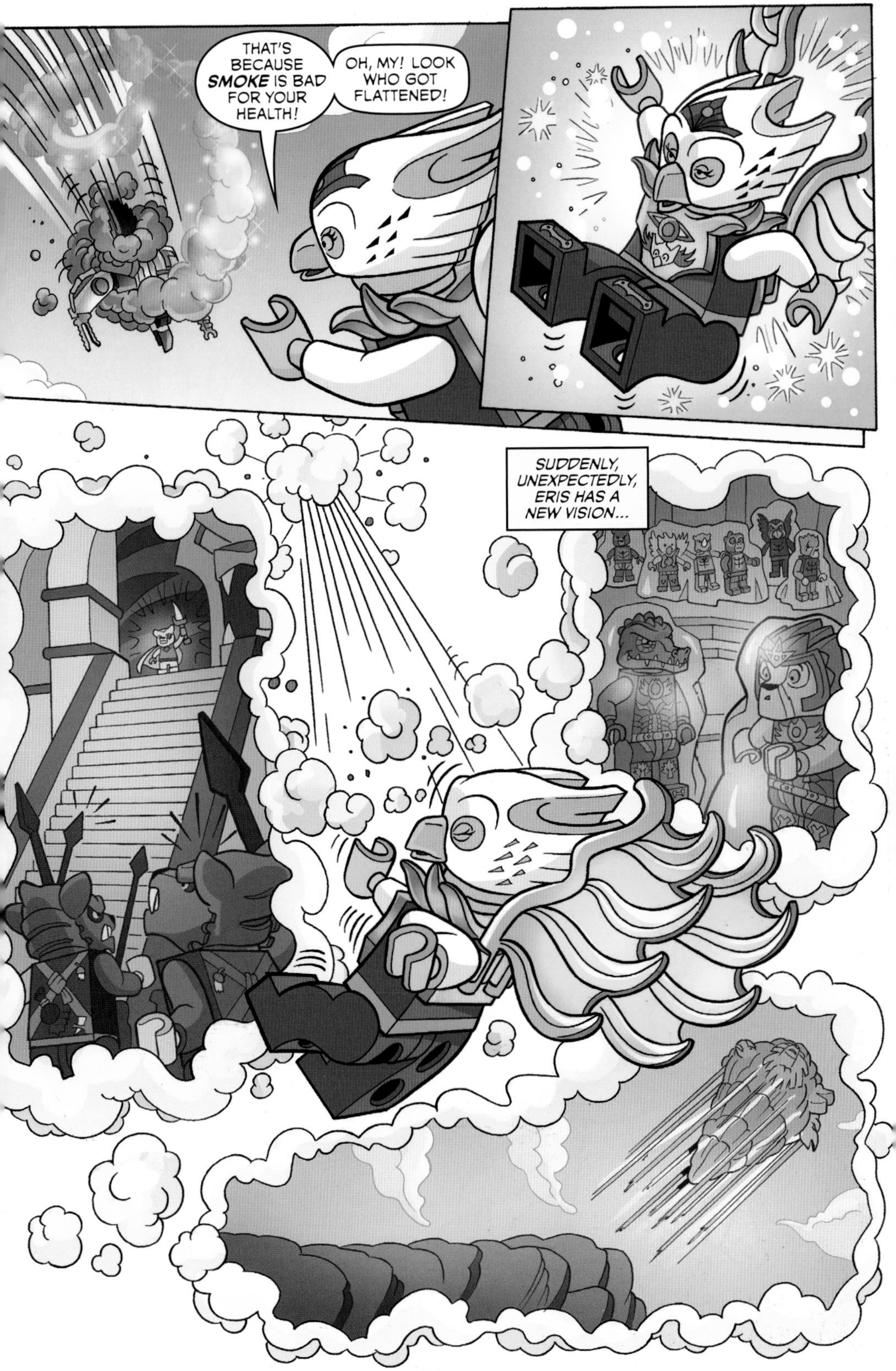
THAT'S BECAUSE SMOKE IS BAD FOR YOUR HEALTH!
OH, MY! LOOK WHO GOT FLATTENED!
SUDDENLY, UNEXPECTEDLY, ERIS HAS A NEW VISION...

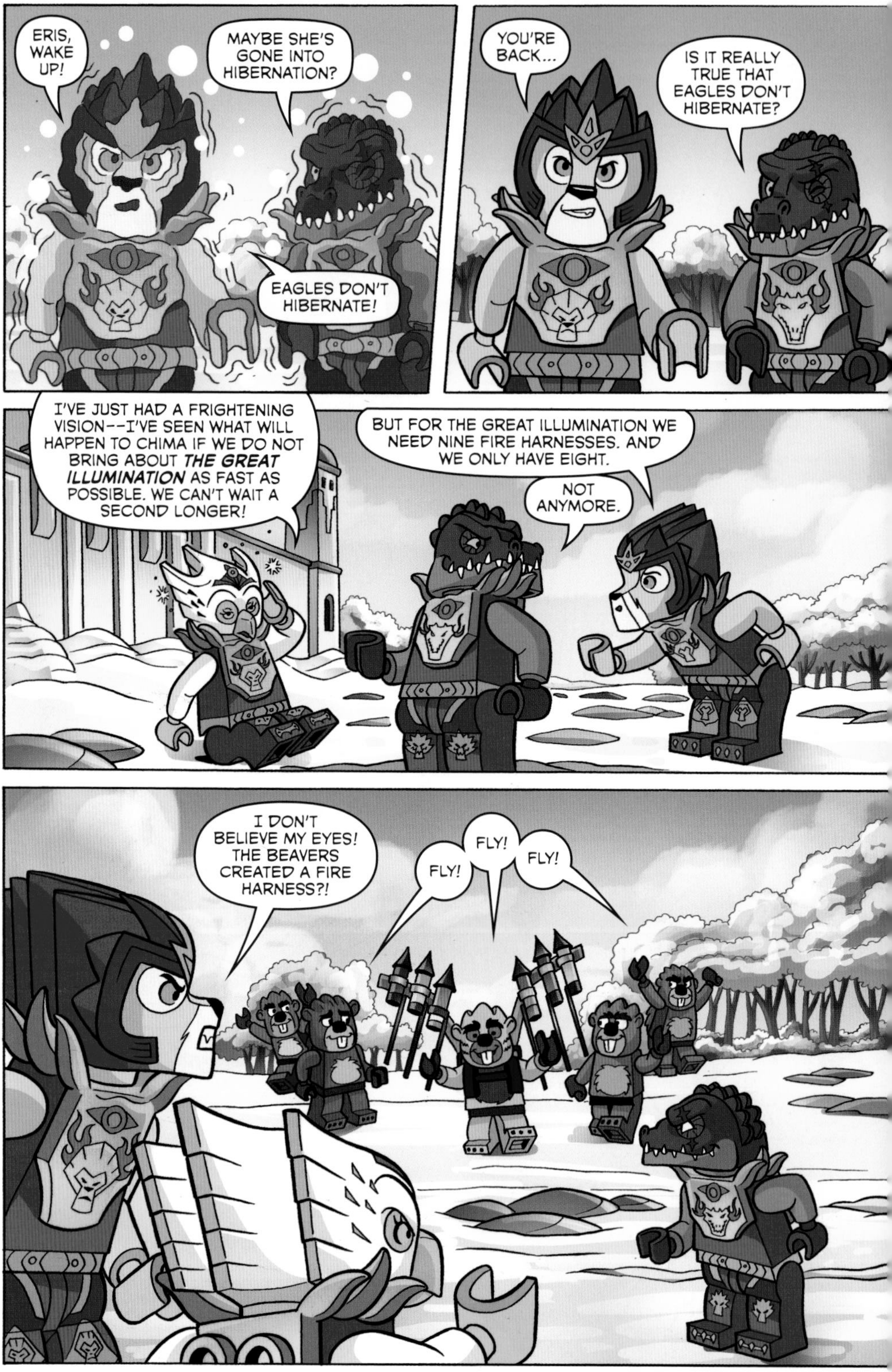
ERIS, WAKE UP!
MAYBE SHE'S GONE INTO HIBERNATION?
EAGLES DON'T HIBERNATE!
YOU'RE BACK...
IS IT REALLY TRUE THAT EAGLES DON'T HIBERNATE?
I'VE JUST HAD A FRIGHTENING VISION--I'VE SEEN WHAT WILL HAPPEN TO CHIMA IF WE DO NOT BRING ABOUT THE GREAT ILLUMINATION AS FAST AS POSSIBLE. WE CAN'T WAIT A SECOND LONGER!
BUT FOR THE GREAT ILLUMINATION WE NEED NINE FIRE HARNESSES. AND WE ONLY HAVE EIGHT.
NOT ANYMORE.
I DON'T BELIEVE MY EYES! THE BEAVERS CREATED A FIRE HARNESS?!
FLY!
FLY!
FLY!

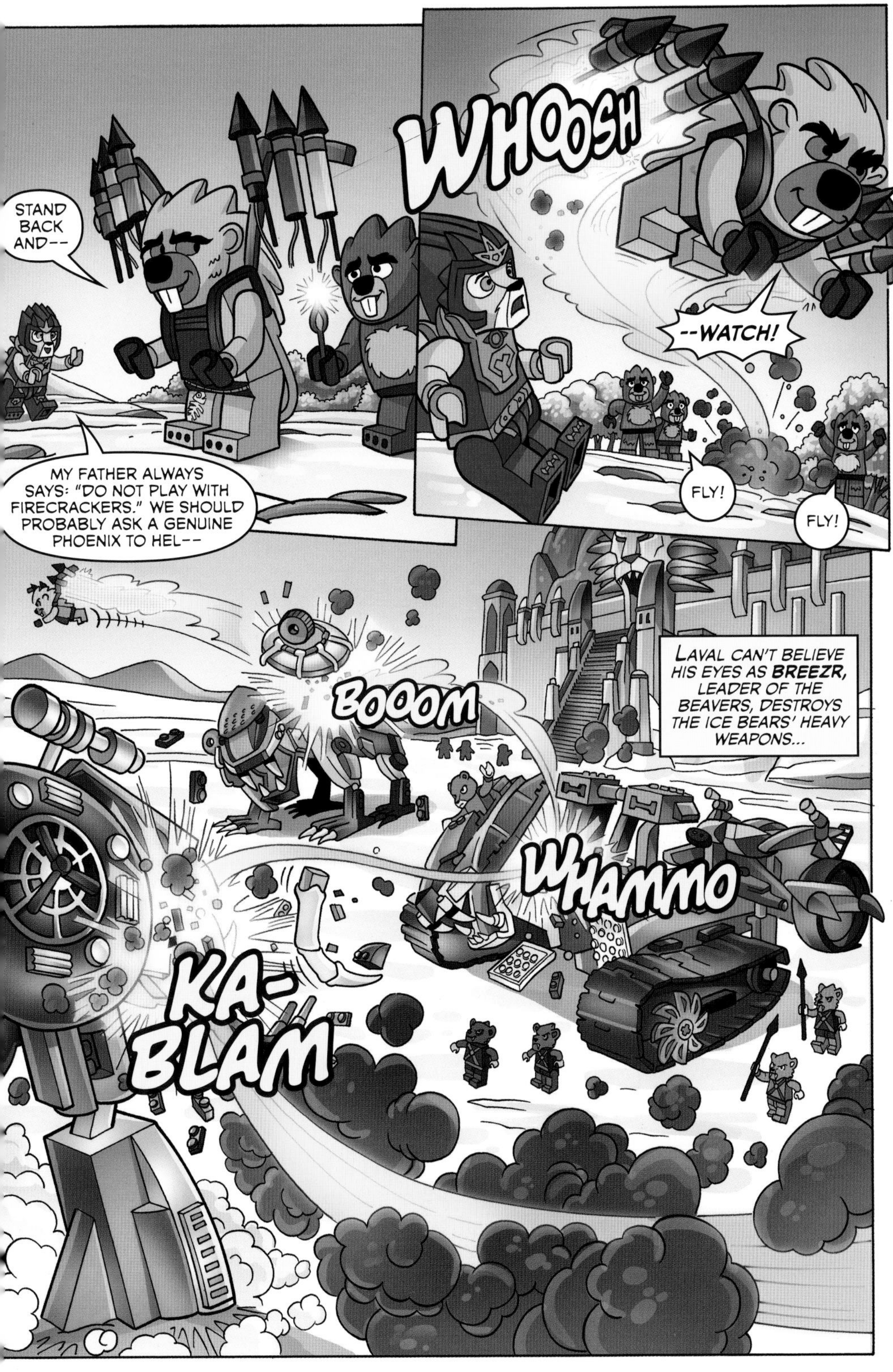
STAND BACK AND--
MY FATHER ALWAYS SAYS: "DO NOT PLAY WITH FIRECRACKERS." WE SHOULD PROBABLY ASK A GENUINE PHOENIX TO HEL--
WHOOSH
--WATCH!
FLY!
FLY!
LAVAL CAN'T BELIEVE HIS EYES AS BREEZR, LEADER OF THE BEAVERS, DESTROYS THE ICE BEARS' HEAVY WEAPONS...
BOOOM
WHAMMO
KA-BLAM

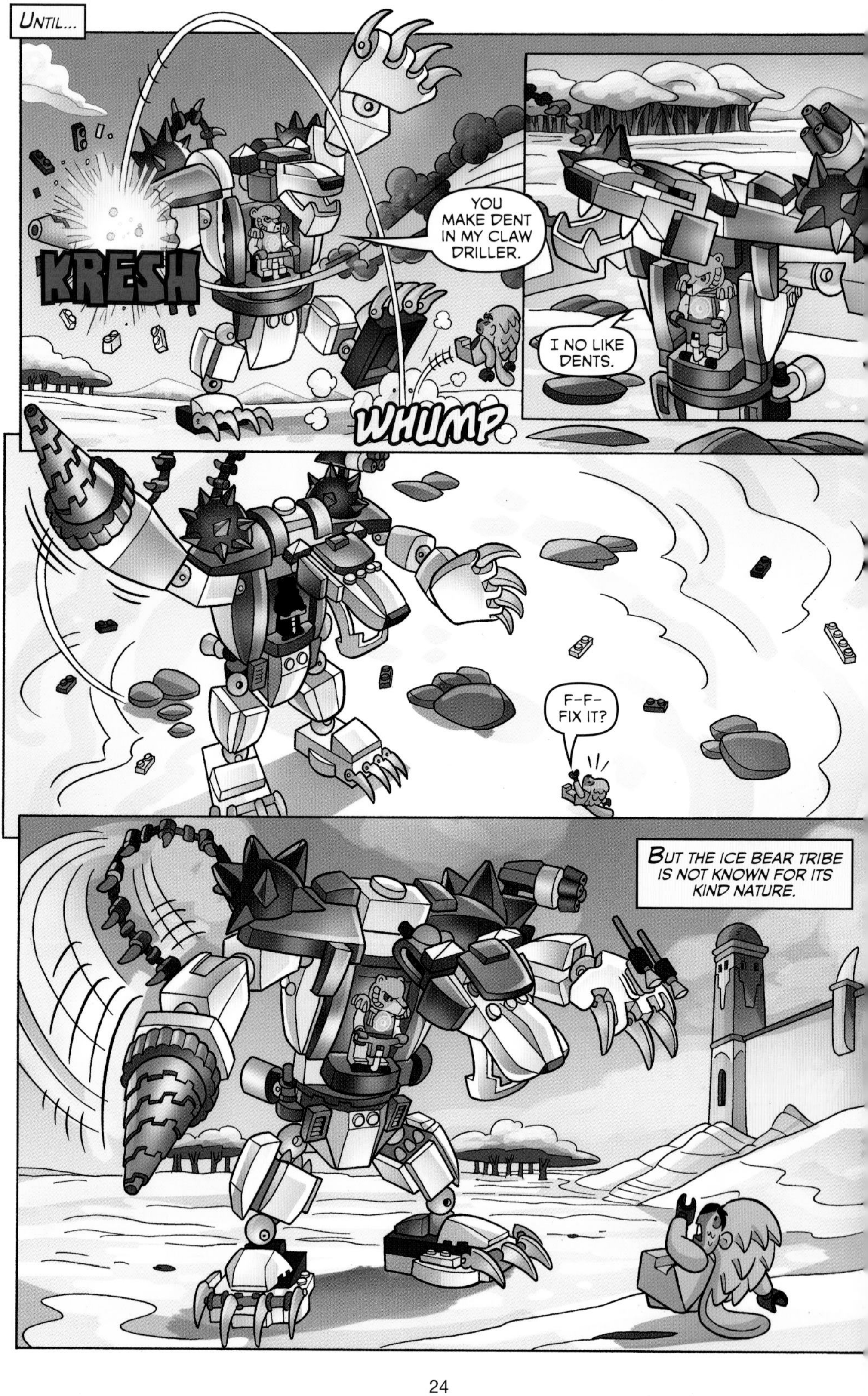
UNTIL...
KRESH
YOU MAKE DENT IN MY CLAW DRILLER.
WHUMP
I NO LIKE DENTS.
F-F-FIX IT?
BUT THE ICE BEAR TRIBE IS NOT KNOWN FOR ITS KIND NATURE.

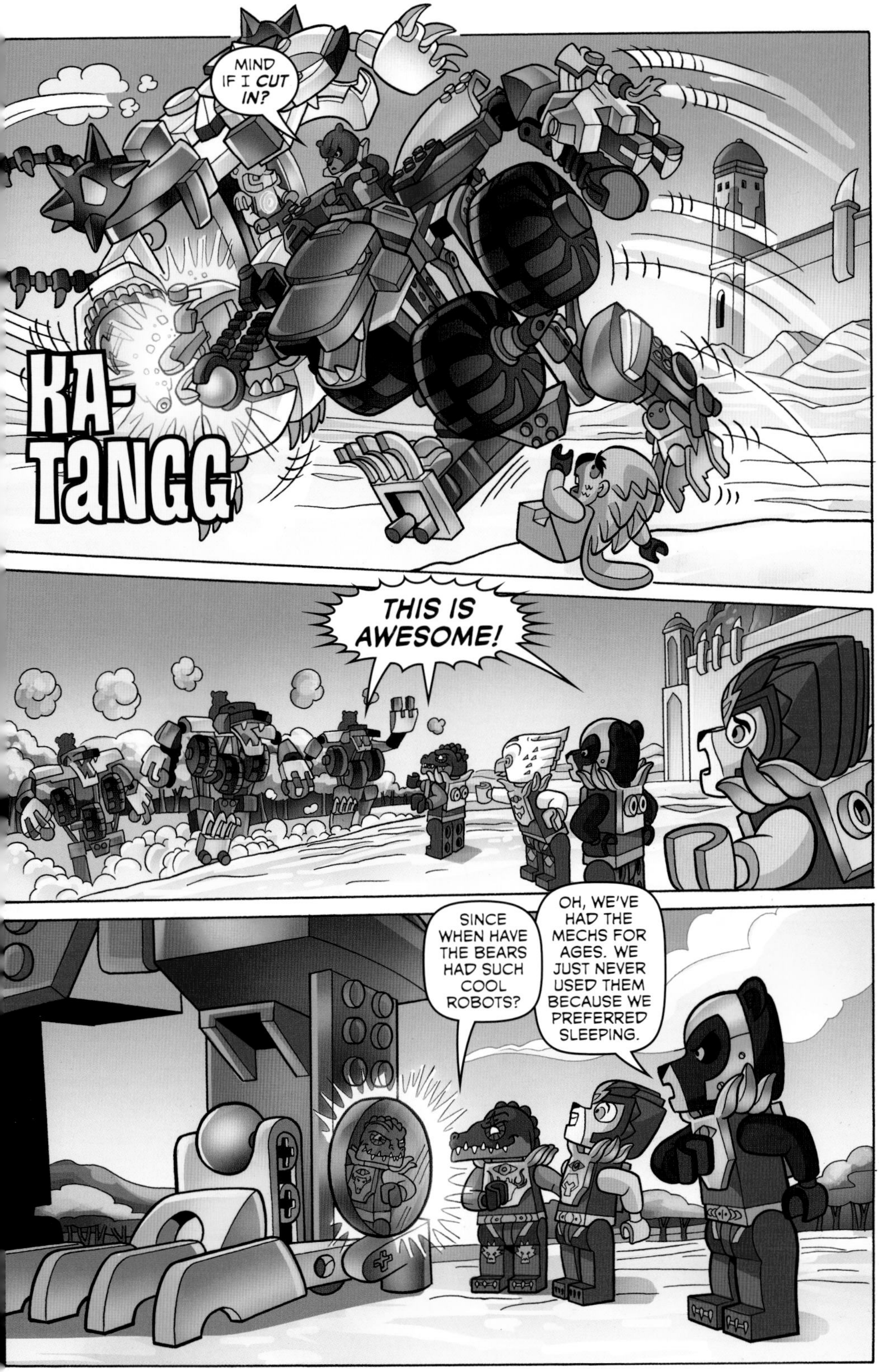
MIND IF I CUT IN?
KA-TANGG
THIS IS AWESOME!
SINCE WHEN HAVE THE BEARS HAD SUCH COOL ROBOTS?
OH, WE'VE HAD THE MECHS FOR AGES. WE JUST NEVER USED THEM BECAUSE WE PREFERRED SLEEPING.

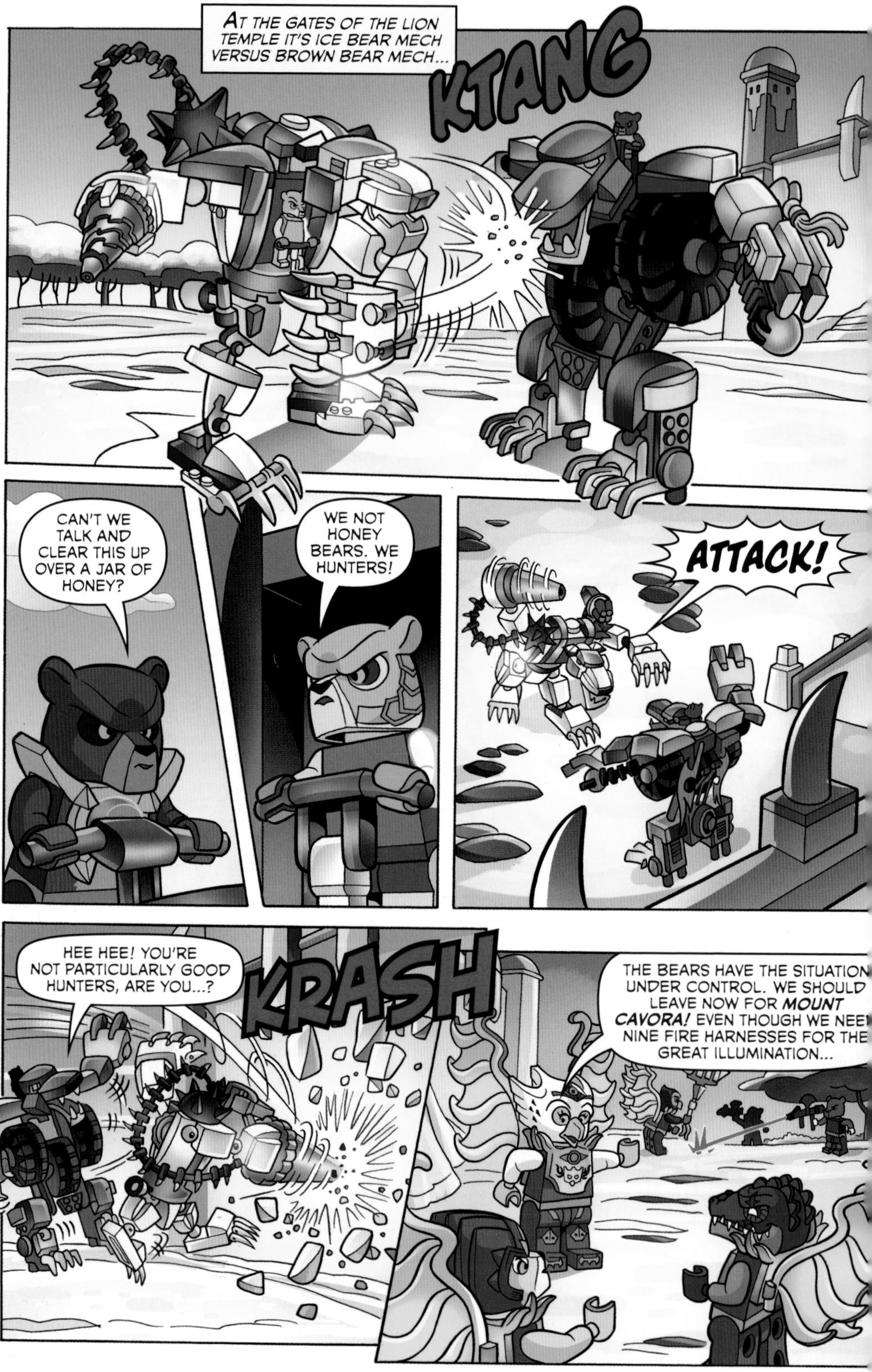

AT THE GATES OF THE LION TEMPLE IT'S ICE BEAR MECH VERSUS BROWN BEAR MECH...
KTANG
CAN'T WE TALK AND CLEAR THIS UP OVER A JAR OF HONEY?
WE NOT HONEY BEARS. WE HUNTERS!
ATTACK!
HEE HEE! YOU'RE NOT PARTICULARLY GOOD HUNTERS, ARE YOU...?
KRASH
THE BEARS HAVE THE SITUATION UNDER CONTROL. WE SHOULD LEAVE NOW FOR *MOUNT CAVORA!* EVEN THOUGH WE NEE NINE FIRE HARNESSES FOR THE GREAT ILLUMINATION...

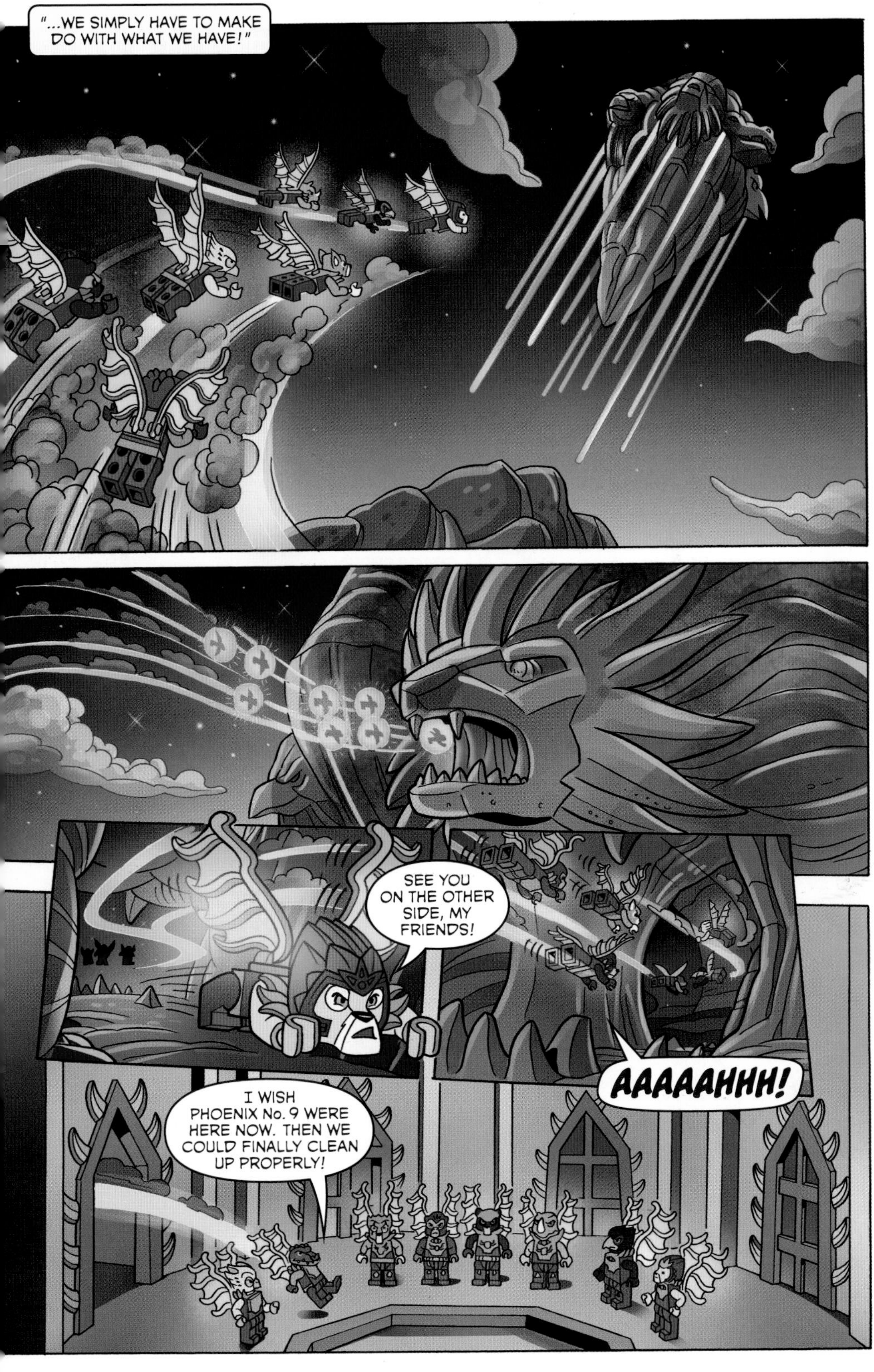
"...WE SIMPLY HAVE TO MAKE DO WITH WHAT WE HAVE!"
SEE YOU ON THE OTHER SIDE, MY FRIENDS!
AAAAAHHH!
I WISH PHOENIX No. 9 WERE HERE NOW. THEN WE COULD FINALLY CLEAN UP PROPERLY!

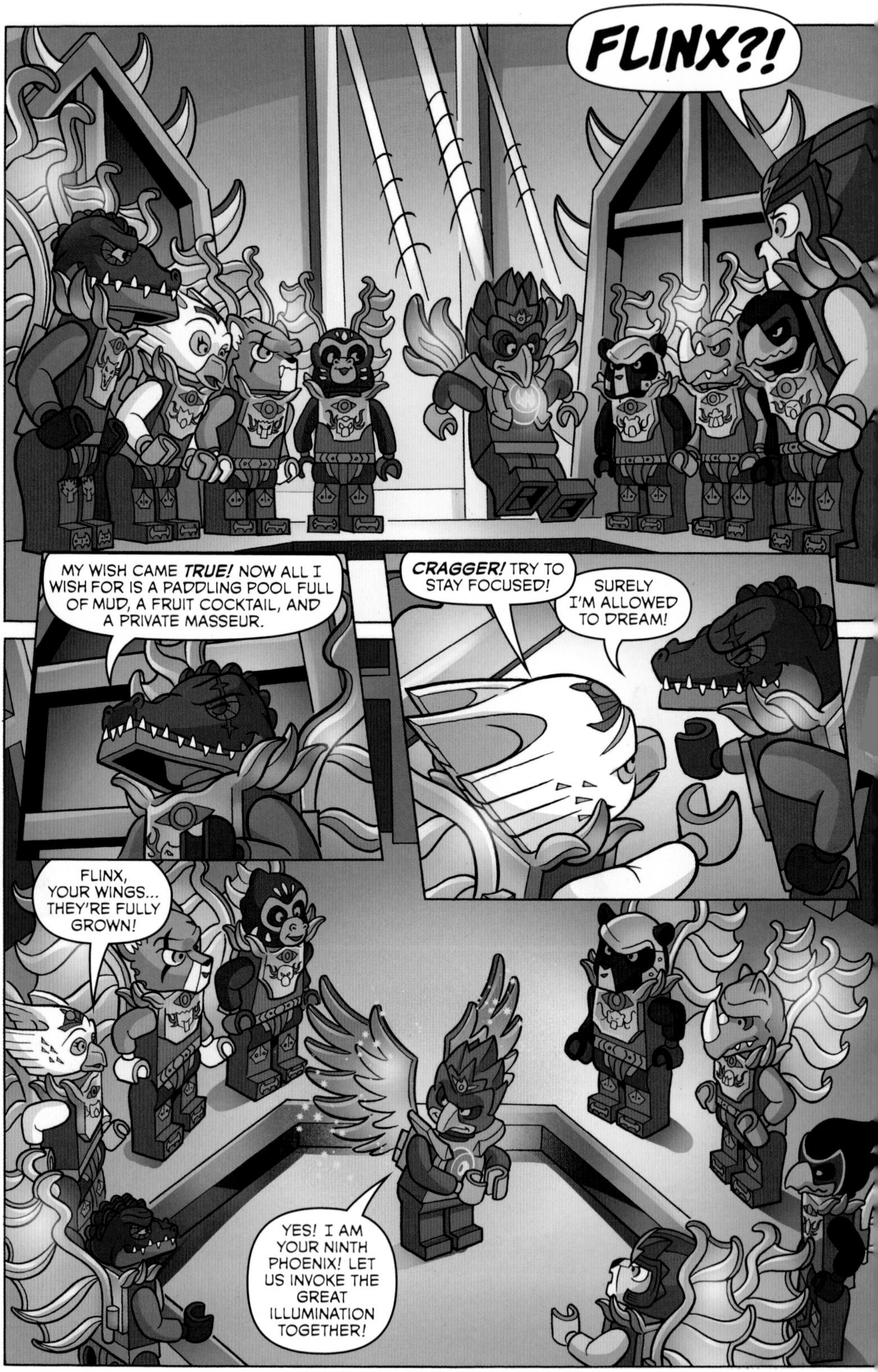
FLINX?!
MY WISH CAME TRUE! NOW ALL I WISH FOR IS A PADDLING POOL FULL OF MUD, A FRUIT COCKTAIL, AND A PRIVATE MASSEUR.
CRAGGER! TRY TO STAY FOCUSED!
SURELY I'M ALLOWED TO DREAM!
FLINX, YOUR WINGS... THEY'RE FULLY GROWN!
YES! I AM YOUR NINTH PHOENIX! LET US INVOKE THE GREAT ILLUMINATION TOGETHER!

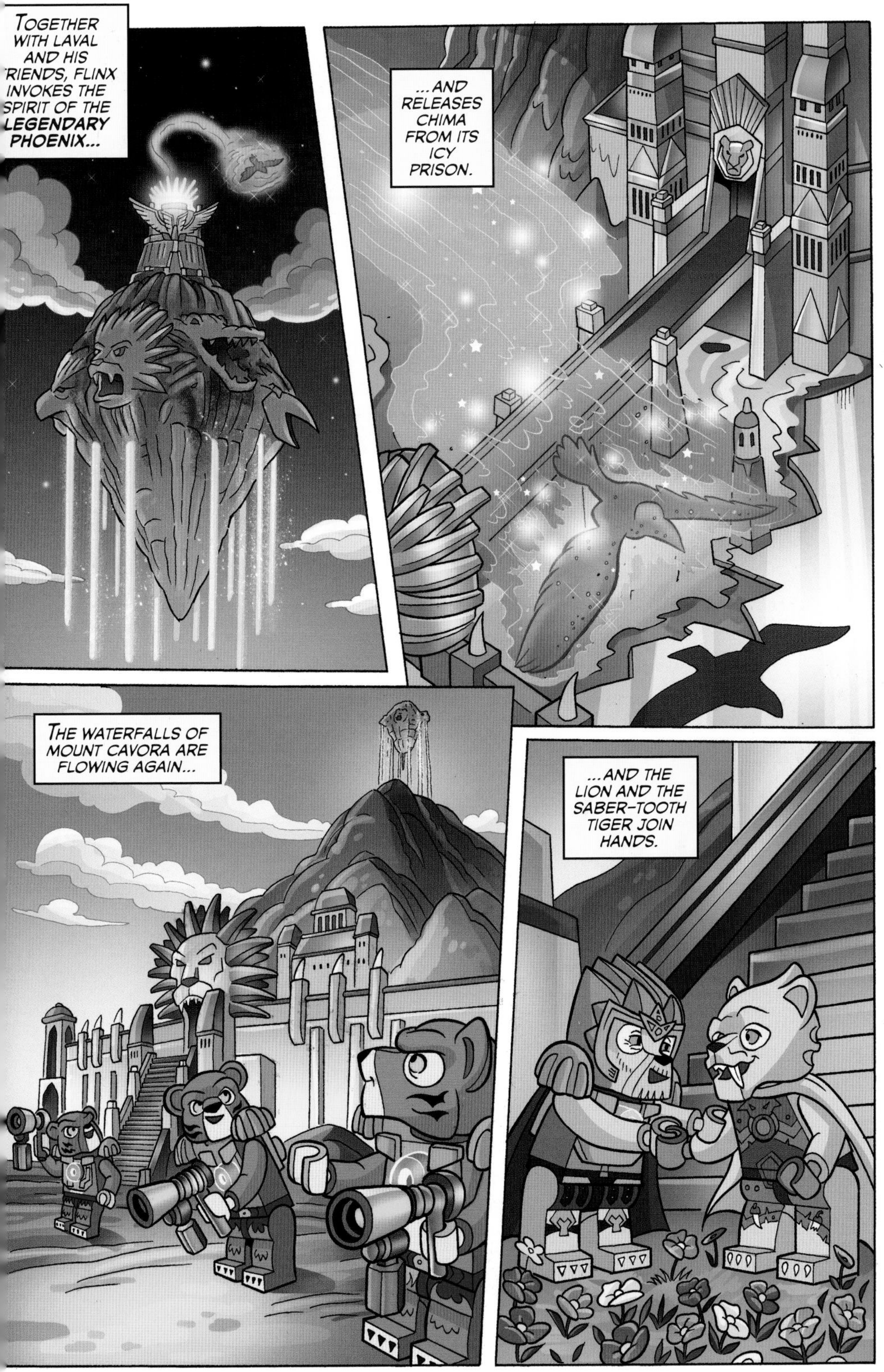
TOGETHER WITH LAVAL AND HIS FRIENDS, FLINX INVOKES THE SPIRIT OF THE LEGENDARY PHOENIX...
...AND RELEASES CHIMA FROM ITS ICY PRISON.
THE WATERFALLS OF MOUNT CAVORA ARE FLOWING AGAIN...
...AND THE LION AND THE SABER-TOOTH TIGER JOIN HANDS.

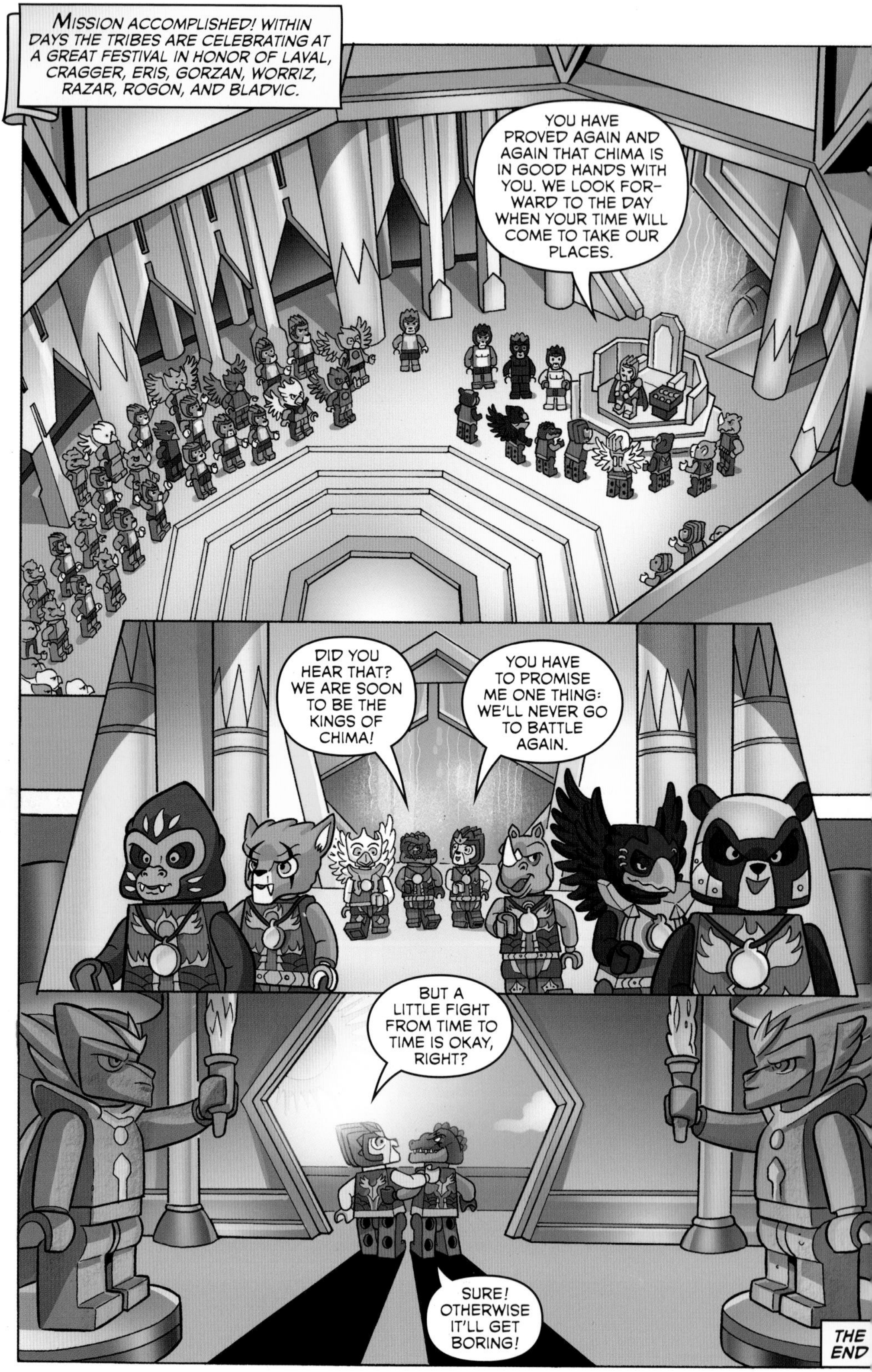
MISSION ACCOMPLISHED! WITHIN DAYS THE TRIBES ARE CELEBRATING AT A GREAT FESTIVAL IN HONOR OF LAVAL, CRAGGER, ERIS, GORZAN, WORRIZ, RAZAR, ROGON, AND BLADVIC.
YOU HAVE PROVED AGAIN AND AGAIN THAT CHIMA IS IN GOOD HANDS WITH YOU. WE LOOK FOR-WARD TO THE DAY WHEN YOUR TIME WILL COME TO TAKE OUR PLACES.
DID YOU HEAR THAT? WE ARE SOON TO BE THE KINGS OF CHIMA!
YOU HAVE TO PROMISE ME ONE THING: WE'LL NEVER GO TO BATTLE AGAIN.
BUT A LITTLE FIGHT FROM TIME TO TIME IS OKAY, RIGHT?
SURE! OTHERWISE IT'LL GET BORING!
THE END

WATCH OUT FOR PAPERCUTZ™

Velcome to the sizzling, yet somewhat shorter sixth and final (this time for sure!) LEGO ® LEGENDS OF HIMA graphic novel, by Yannick Grotholt and Comicon, from Papercutz—those CHI-loving men and women edicated to publishing great graphic novels for all ages. I'm Jim Salicrup, the slightly sobbing Editor-in-Chief nd Greatly Illuminated! Why am I gently weeping? As George Harrison once sang, "All Things Must Pass," nd unfortunately that applies to this series of LEGO LEGENDS OF CHIMA graphic novels as well. If you've ead this column in the last two graphic novels, this won't be a surprise. We even thought it was all over with ne fourth graphic novel, but the news of the LEGO LEGENDS OF CHIMA graphic novel series' end was a tad remature, and we survived for two more graphic novels. But, I'm afraid this is it.

ut while Papercutz will no longer be publishing any new LEGO LEGENDS OF CHIMA graphic novels, we are ublishing more exciting stuff than ever before. Just check us out on Papercutz.com for an idea of what other ool graphic novels we'll be publishing. Here's a short list of just the first few (A-C!) that are available now:

Emmanuel Guibert
Marc Boutavant
ARiOL
Top Dog
PAPERCUTZ

Ariol © Bayard Editions

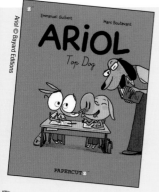

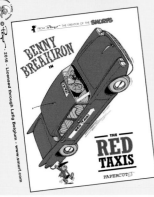

ANNOYING ORANGE – Based on the Internet sensation, enjoy comics by master cartoonists Mike Kazaleh and Scott Shaw!

ARIOL – He's just a donkey like you and me! This series is perfect for anyone who either is a kid or has been a kid at some point. Written by Emmanuel Guibert and drawn by Marc Boutavant.

BENNY BREAKIRON – From Peyo, the creator of the Smurfs comes a super-powered little French boy!

FROM Peyo THE CREATOR OF THE SMURFS
BENNY BREAKIRON
IN
THE RED TAXIS
PAPERCUTZ

© Peyo - 2016 - Licensed through Lafig Belgium - www.smurf.com

BREADWINNERS – Based on the hit Nickelodeon animated series. See SwaySway and Buhdeuce deliver bread in their rocket van. Written by Stefan Petrucha and drawn by Allison Strejlau and Mike Kazaleh. (And don't forget NICKELODEON MAGAZINE and the SANJAY AND CRAIG, HARVEY BEAKS, and PIG GOAT BANANA CRICKET graphic novels we mentioned in CHIMA #5.)

CLASSICS ILLUSTRATED and CLASSICS ILLUSTRATED DELUXE – Featuring Stories by the World's Greatest Authors!

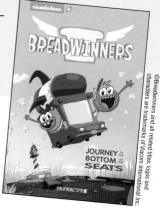

nickelodeon
BREADWINNERS
JOURNEY TO THE BOTTOM OF THE SEATS
PAPERCUTZ

©Breadwinners and all related titles, logos and characters are trademarks of Viacom International Inc.

ust to be perfectly clear, while Papercutz may not be publishing any urther new LEGO LEGENDS OF CHIMA graphic novels, there are still lenty of new LEGO LEGENDS OF CHIMA products coming your way! ust keep an eye on LEGO.com for all the latest big announcements!

o while this is indeed the final graphic novel, clearly with everything apercutz and LEGO has planned for the future, it's safe to say, that's ot all, folks—the best is yet to come!

Thanks,

Jim

STAY IN TOUCH!

EMAIL:	salicrup@papercutz.com
WEB:	papercutz.com
TWITTER:	@papercutzgn
FACEBOOK:	PAPERCUTZGRAPHICNOVELS
FAN MAIL:	Papercutz, 160 Broadway, Suite 700, East Wing, New York, NY 10038

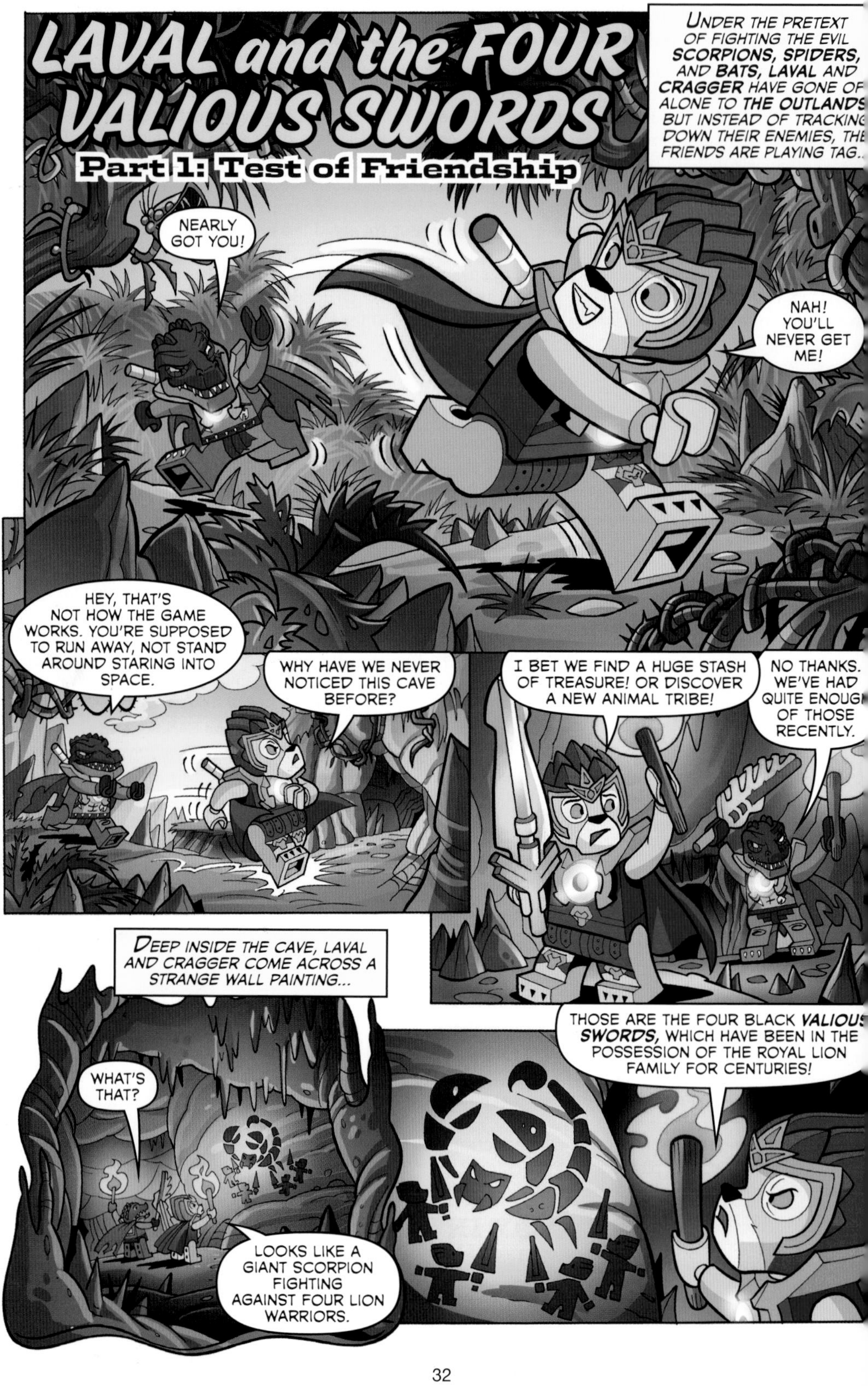
LAVAL and the FOUR VALIOUS SWORDS
Part 1: Test of Friendship
UNDER THE PRETEXT OF FIGHTING THE EVIL SCORPIONS, SPIDERS, AND BATS, LAVAL AND CRAGGER HAVE GONE OF ALONE TO THE OUTLANDS BUT INSTEAD OF TRACKING DOWN THEIR ENEMIES, THE FRIENDS ARE PLAYING TAG...
NEARLY GOT YOU!
NAH! YOU'LL NEVER GET ME!
HEY, THAT'S NOT HOW THE GAME WORKS. YOU'RE SUPPOSED TO RUN AWAY, NOT STAND AROUND STARING INTO SPACE.
WHY HAVE WE NEVER NOTICED THIS CAVE BEFORE?
I BET WE FIND A HUGE STASH OF TREASURE! OR DISCOVER A NEW ANIMAL TRIBE!
NO THANKS. WE'VE HAD QUITE ENOUG OF THOSE RECENTLY.
DEEP INSIDE THE CAVE, LAVAL AND CRAGGER COME ACROSS A STRANGE WALL PAINTING...
WHAT'S THAT?
LOOKS LIKE A GIANT SCORPION FIGHTING AGAINST FOUR LION WARRIORS.
THOSE ARE THE FOUR BLACK VALIOUS SWORDS, WHICH HAVE BEEN IN THE POSSESSION OF THE ROYAL LION FAMILY FOR CENTURIES!

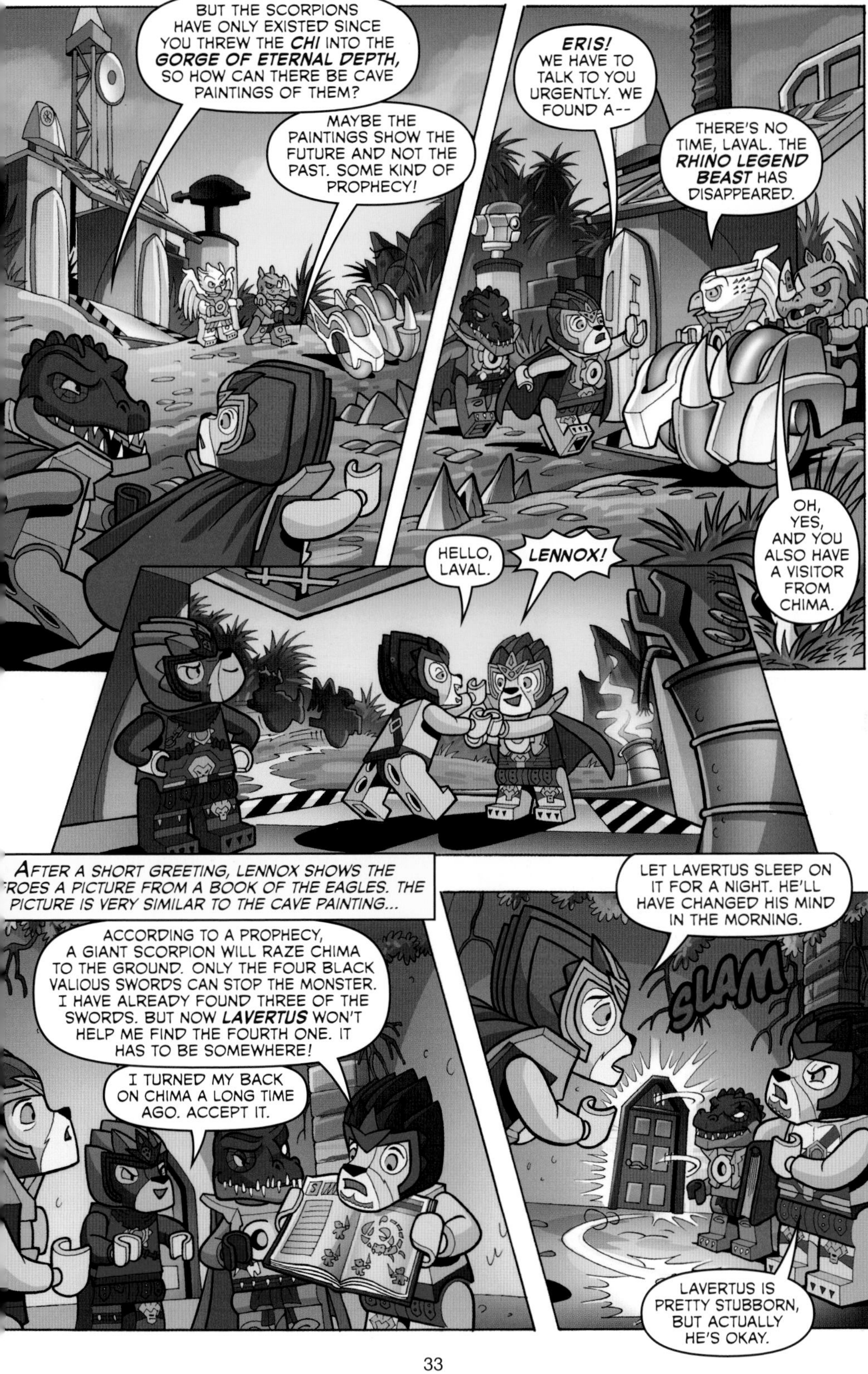

BUT THE SCORPIONS HAVE ONLY EXISTED SINCE YOU THREW THE *CHI* INTO THE *GORGE OF ETERNAL DEPTH*, SO HOW CAN THERE BE CAVE PAINTINGS OF THEM?
MAYBE THE PAINTINGS SHOW THE FUTURE AND NOT THE PAST. SOME KIND OF PROPHECY!
ERIS! WE HAVE TO TALK TO YOU URGENTLY. WE FOUND A--
THERE'S NO TIME, LAVAL. THE *RHINO LEGEND BEAST* HAS DISAPPEARED.
OH, YES, AND YOU ALSO HAVE A VISITOR FROM CHIMA.
HELLO, LAVAL.
LENNOX!
AFTER A SHORT GREETING, LENNOX SHOWS THE *ROES A PICTURE FROM A BOOK OF THE EAGLES. THE PICTURE IS VERY SIMILAR TO THE CAVE PAINTING...*
ACCORDING TO A PROPHECY, A GIANT SCORPION WILL RAZE CHIMA TO THE GROUND. ONLY THE FOUR BLACK VALIOUS SWORDS CAN STOP THE MONSTER. I HAVE ALREADY FOUND THREE OF THE SWORDS. BUT NOW *LAVERTUS* WON'T HELP ME FIND THE FOURTH ONE. IT HAS TO BE SOMEWHERE!
I TURNED MY BACK ON CHIMA A LONG TIME AGO. ACCEPT IT.
LET LAVERTUS SLEEP ON IT FOR A NIGHT. HE'LL HAVE CHANGED HIS MIND IN THE MORNING.
SLAM
LAVERTUS IS PRETTY STUBBORN, BUT ACTUALLY HE'S OKAY.

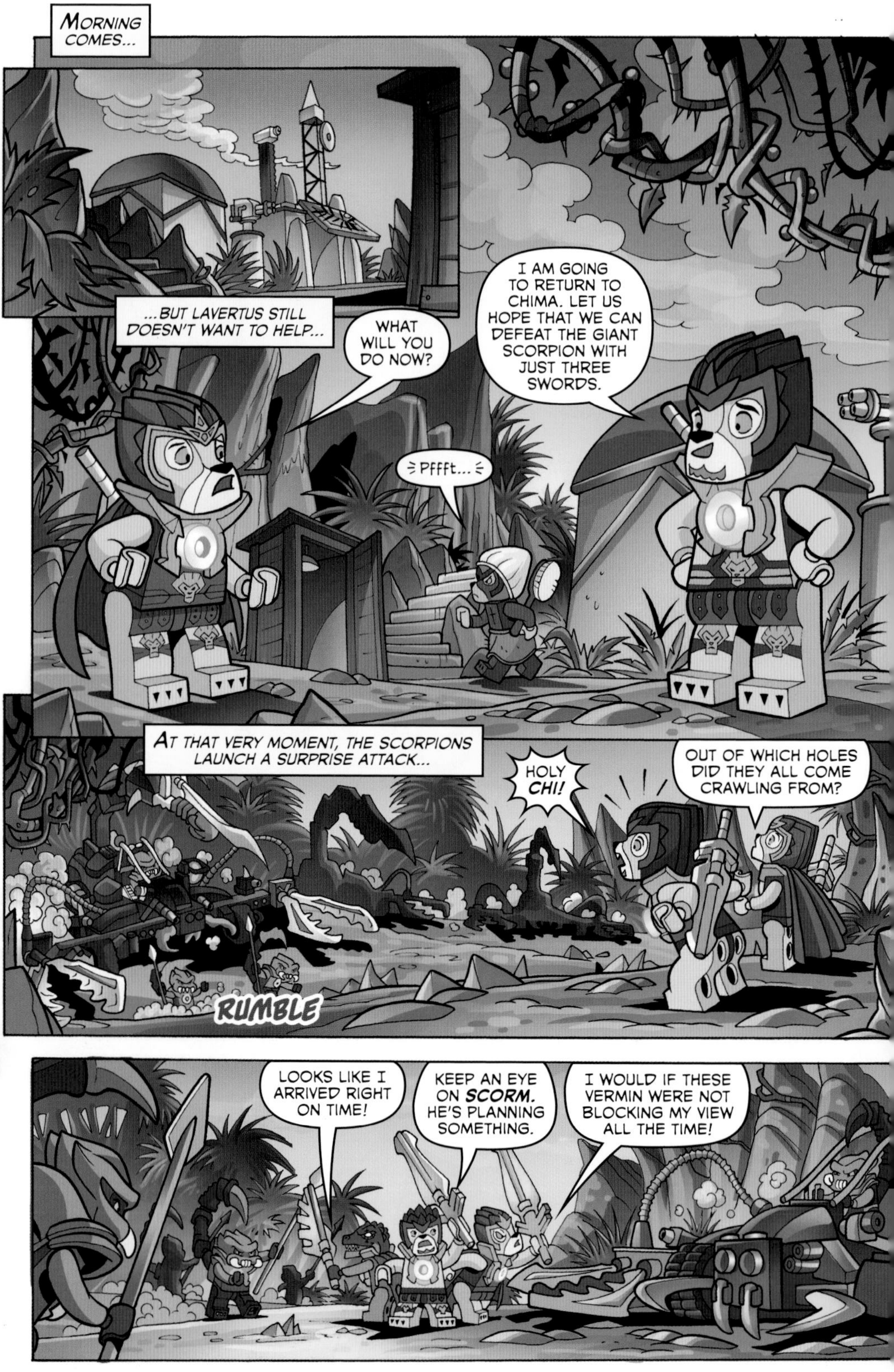
MORNING COMES...
...BUT LAVERTUS STILL DOESN'T WANT TO HELP...
WHAT WILL YOU DO NOW?
I AM GOING TO RETURN TO CHIMA. LET US HOPE THAT WE CAN DEFEAT THE GIANT SCORPION WITH JUST THREE SWORDS.
PFFFt...
AT THAT VERY MOMENT, THE SCORPIONS LAUNCH A SURPRISE ATTACK...
HOLY CHI!
OUT OF WHICH HOLES DID THEY ALL COME CRAWLING FROM?
RUMBLE
LOOKS LIKE I ARRIVED RIGHT ON TIME!
KEEP AN EYE ON SCORM. HE'S PLANNING SOMETHING.
I WOULD IF THESE VERMIN WERE NOT BLOCKING MY VIEW ALL THE TIME!

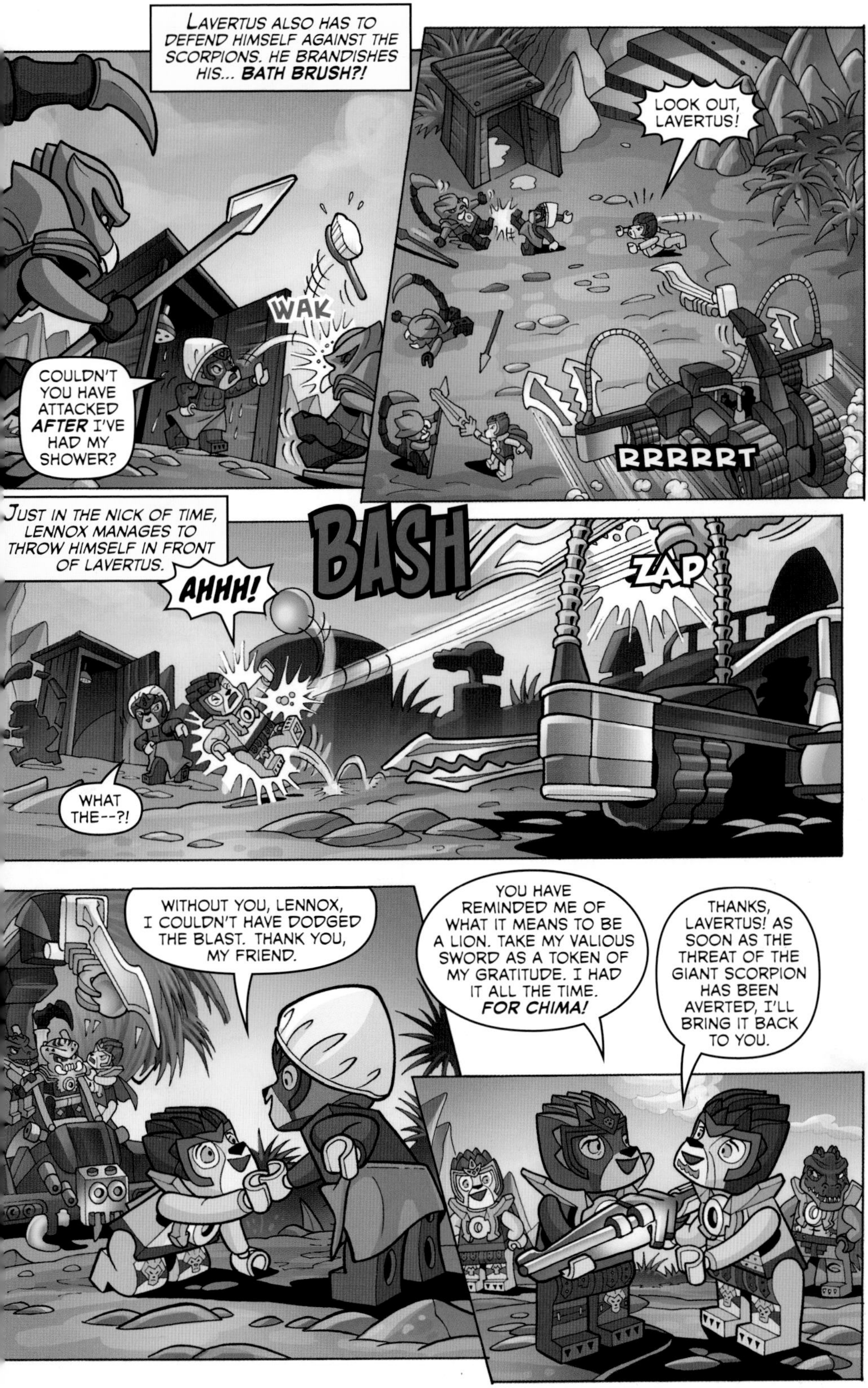
LAVERTUS ALSO HAS TO DEFEND HIMSELF AGAINST THE SCORPIONS. HE BRANDISHES HIS... **BATH BRUSH?!**
WAK
COULDN'T YOU HAVE ATTACKED **AFTER** I'VE HAD MY SHOWER?
LOOK OUT, LAVERTUS!
RRRRRT
JUST IN THE NICK OF TIME, LENNOX MANAGES TO THROW HIMSELF IN FRONT OF LAVERTUS.
BASH
AHHH!
ZAP
WHAT THE--?!
WITHOUT YOU, LENNOX, I COULDN'T HAVE DODGED THE BLAST. THANK YOU, MY FRIEND.
YOU HAVE REMINDED ME OF WHAT IT MEANS TO BE A LION. TAKE MY VALIOUS SWORD AS A TOKEN OF MY GRATITUDE. I HAD IT ALL THE TIME. **FOR CHIMA!**
THANKS, LAVERTUS! AS SOON AS THE THREAT OF THE GIANT SCORPION HAS BEEN AVERTED, I'LL BRING IT BACK TO YOU.

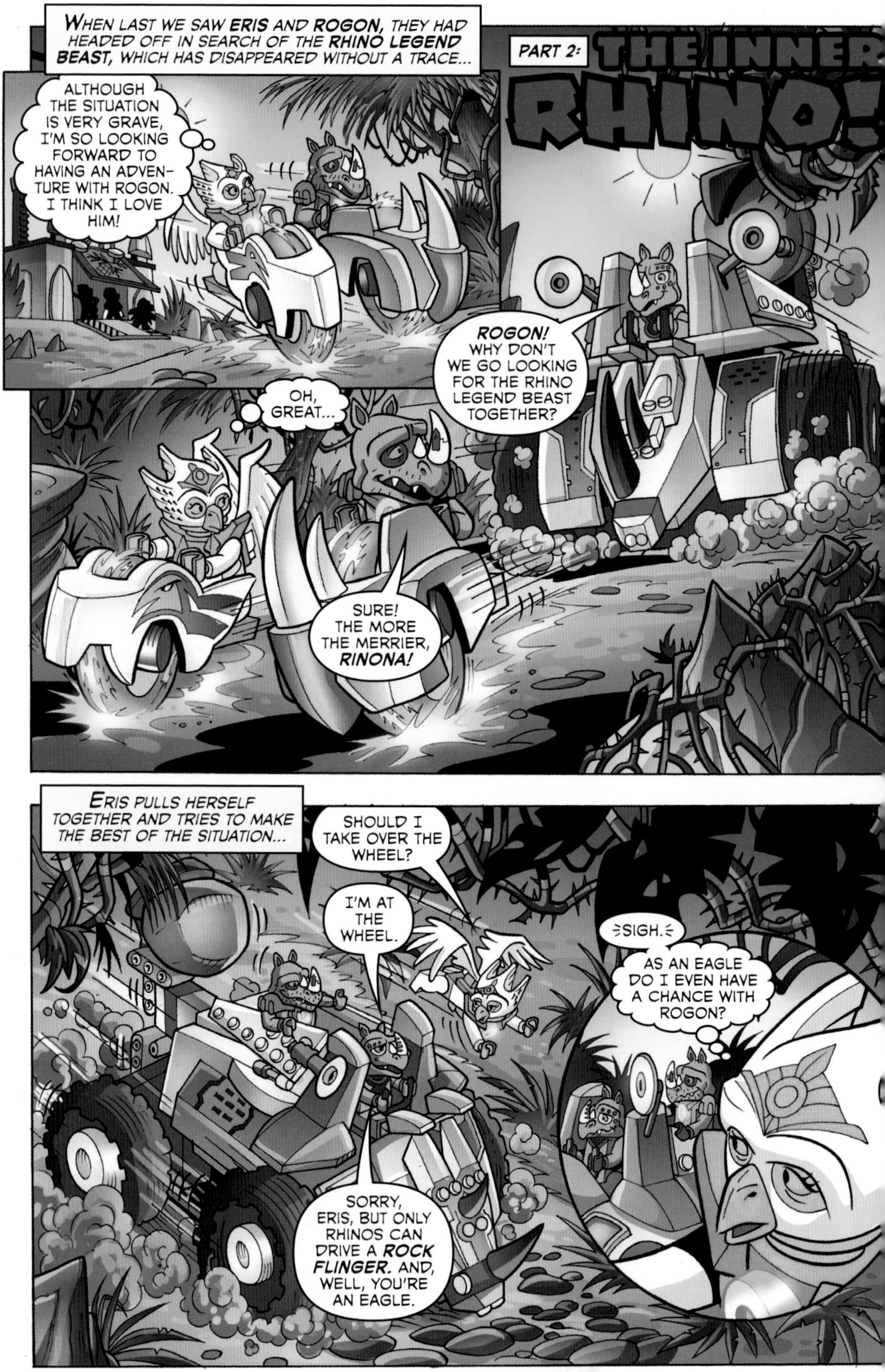
WHEN LAST WE SAW ERIS AND ROGON, THEY HAD HEADED OFF IN SEARCH OF THE RHINO LEGEND BEAST, WHICH HAS DISAPPEARED WITHOUT A TRACE...
PART 2: THE INNER RHINO!
ALTHOUGH THE SITUATION IS VERY GRAVE, I'M SO LOOKING FORWARD TO HAVING AN ADVEN-TURE WITH ROGON. I THINK I LOVE HIM!
ROGON! WHY DON'T WE GO LOOKING FOR THE RHINO LEGEND BEAST TOGETHER?
OH, GREAT...
SURE! THE MORE THE MERRIER, RINONA!
ERIS PULLS HERSELF TOGETHER AND TRIES TO MAKE THE BEST OF THE SITUATION...
SHOULD I TAKE OVER THE WHEEL?
I'M AT THE WHEEL.
SIGH.
AS AN EAGLE DO I EVEN HAVE A CHANCE WITH ROGON?
SORRY, ERIS, BUT ONLY RHINOS CAN DRIVE A ROCK FLINGER. AND, WELL, YOU'RE AN EAGLE.

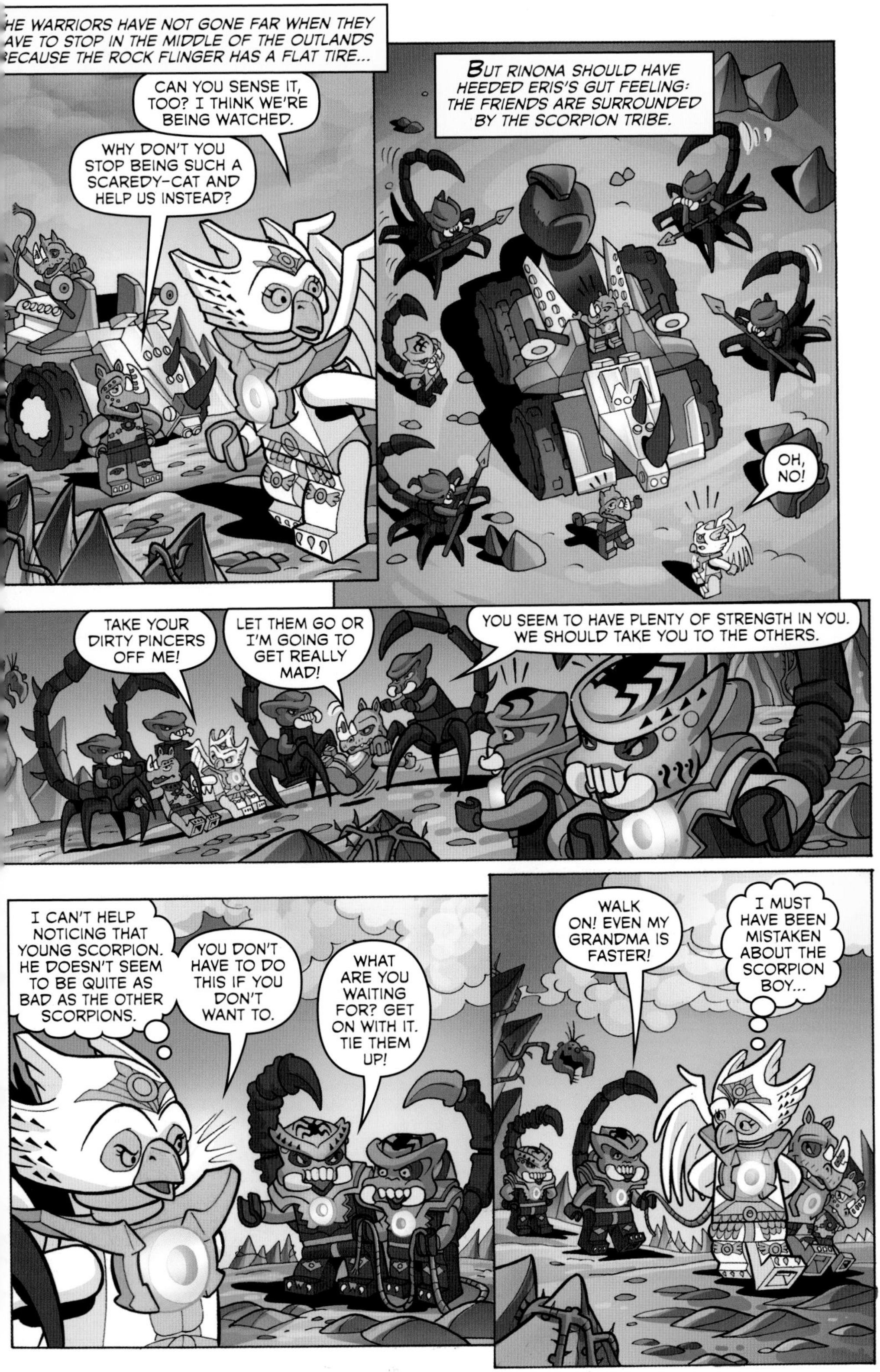
HE WARRIORS HAVE NOT GONE FAR WHEN THEY AVE TO STOP IN THE MIDDLE OF THE OUTLANDS ECAUSE THE ROCK FLINGER HAS A FLAT TIRE...
CAN YOU SENSE IT, TOO? I THINK WE'RE BEING WATCHED.
WHY DON'T YOU STOP BEING SUCH A SCAREDY-CAT AND HELP US INSTEAD?
BUT RINONA SHOULD HAVE HEEDED ERIS'S GUT FEELING: THE FRIENDS ARE SURROUNDED BY THE SCORPION TRIBE.
OH, NO!
TAKE YOUR DIRTY PINCERS OFF ME!
LET THEM GO OR I'M GOING TO GET REALLY MAD!
YOU SEEM TO HAVE PLENTY OF STRENGTH IN YOU. WE SHOULD TAKE YOU TO THE OTHERS.
I CAN'T HELP NOTICING THAT YOUNG SCORPION. HE DOESN'T SEEM TO BE QUITE AS BAD AS THE OTHER SCORPIONS.
YOU DON'T HAVE TO DO THIS IF YOU DON'T WANT TO.
WHAT ARE YOU WAITING FOR? GET ON WITH IT. TIE THEM UP!
WALK ON! EVEN MY GRANDMA IS FASTER!
I MUST HAVE BEEN MISTAKEN ABOUT THE SCORPION BOY...

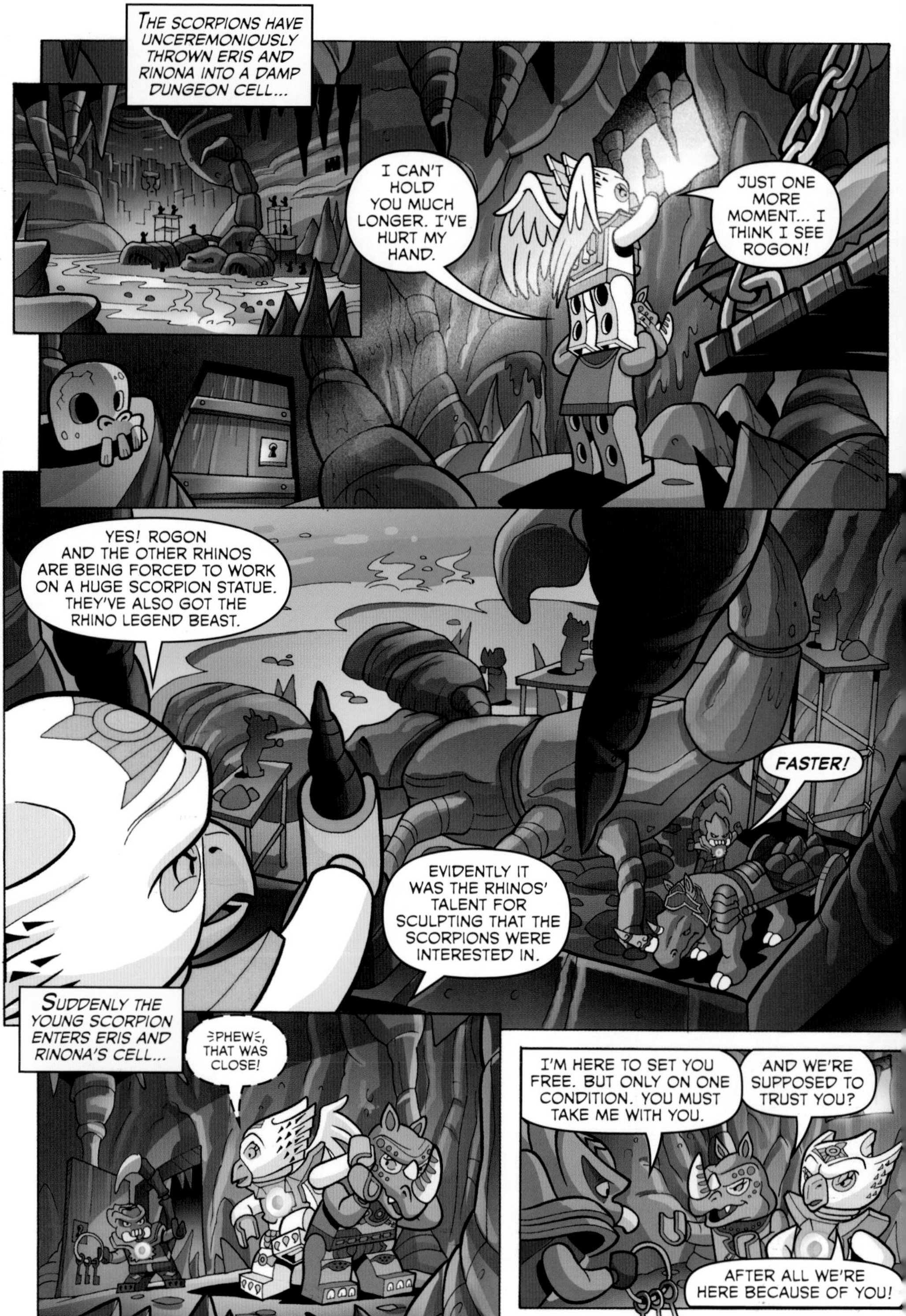
THE SCORPIONS HAVE UNCEREMONIOUSLY THROWN ERIS AND RINONA INTO A DAMP DUNGEON CELL...
I CAN'T HOLD YOU MUCH LONGER. I'VE HURT MY HAND.
JUST ONE MORE MOMENT... I THINK I SEE ROGON!
YES! ROGON AND THE OTHER RHINOS ARE BEING FORCED TO WORK ON A HUGE SCORPION STATUE. THEY'VE ALSO GOT THE RHINO LEGEND BEAST.
FASTER!
EVIDENTLY IT WAS THE RHINOS' TALENT FOR SCULPTING THAT THE SCORPIONS WERE INTERESTED IN.
SUDDENLY THE YOUNG SCORPION ENTERS ERIS AND RINONA'S CELL...
PHEW, THAT WAS CLOSE!
I'M HERE TO SET YOU FREE. BUT ONLY ON ONE CONDITION. YOU MUST TAKE ME WITH YOU.
AND WE'RE SUPPOSED TO TRUST YOU?
AFTER ALL WE'RE HERE BECAUSE OF YOU!

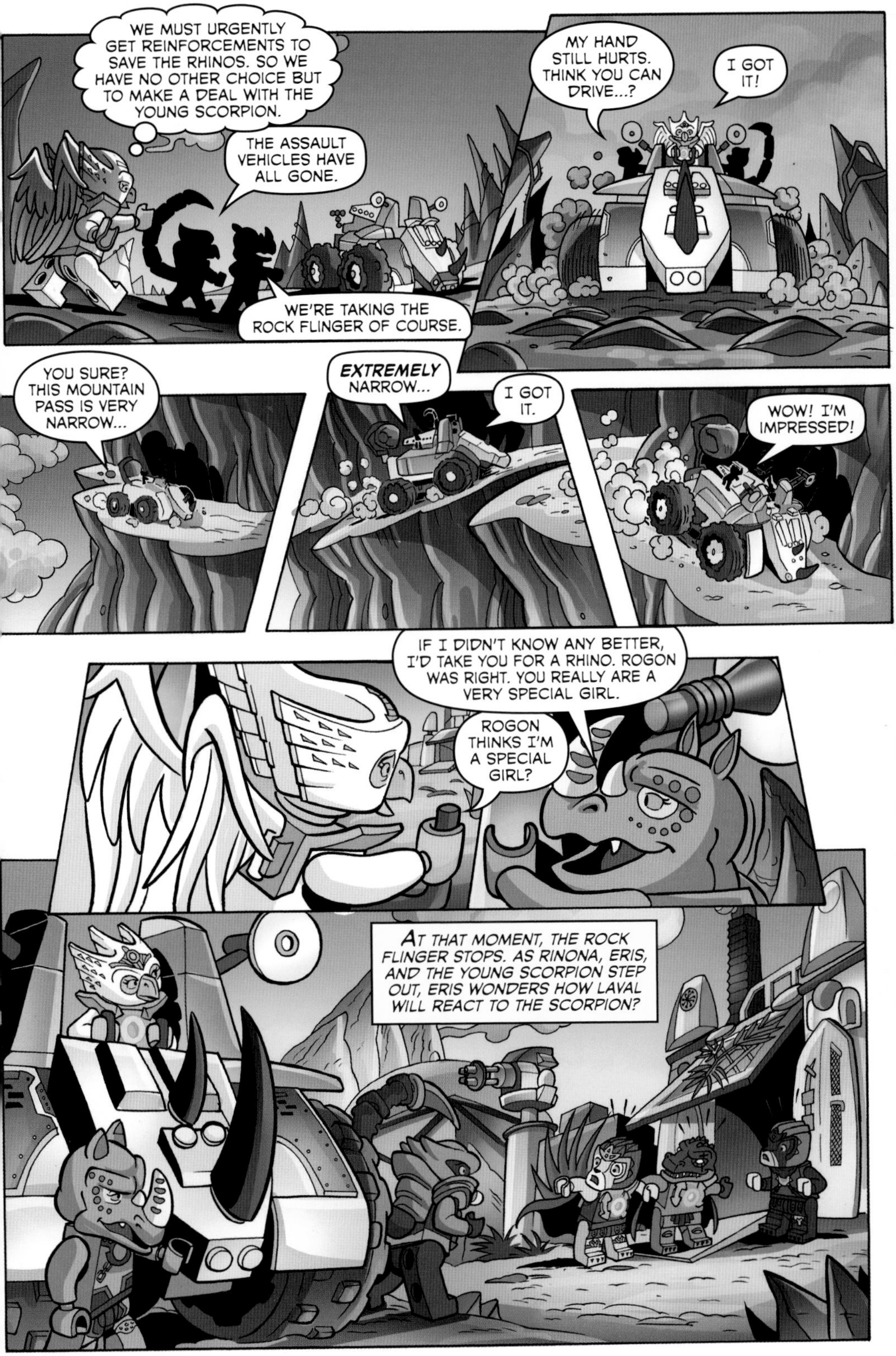
WE MUST URGENTLY GET REINFORCEMENTS TO SAVE THE RHINOS. SO WE HAVE NO OTHER CHOICE BUT TO MAKE A DEAL WITH THE YOUNG SCORPION.
THE ASSAULT VEHICLES HAVE ALL GONE.
WE'RE TAKING THE ROCK FLINGER OF COURSE.
MY HAND STILL HURTS. THINK YOU CAN DRIVE...?
I GOT IT!
YOU SURE? THIS MOUNTAIN PASS IS VERY NARROW...
EXTREMELY NARROW...
I GOT IT.
WOW! I'M IMPRESSED!
IF I DIDN'T KNOW ANY BETTER, I'D TAKE YOU FOR A RHINO. ROGON WAS RIGHT. YOU REALLY ARE A VERY SPECIAL GIRL.
ROGON THINKS I'M A SPECIAL GIRL?
AT THAT MOMENT, THE ROCK FLINGER STOPS. AS RINONA, ERIS, AND THE YOUNG SCORPION STEP OUT, ERIS WONDERS HOW LAVAL WILL REACT TO THE SCORPION?

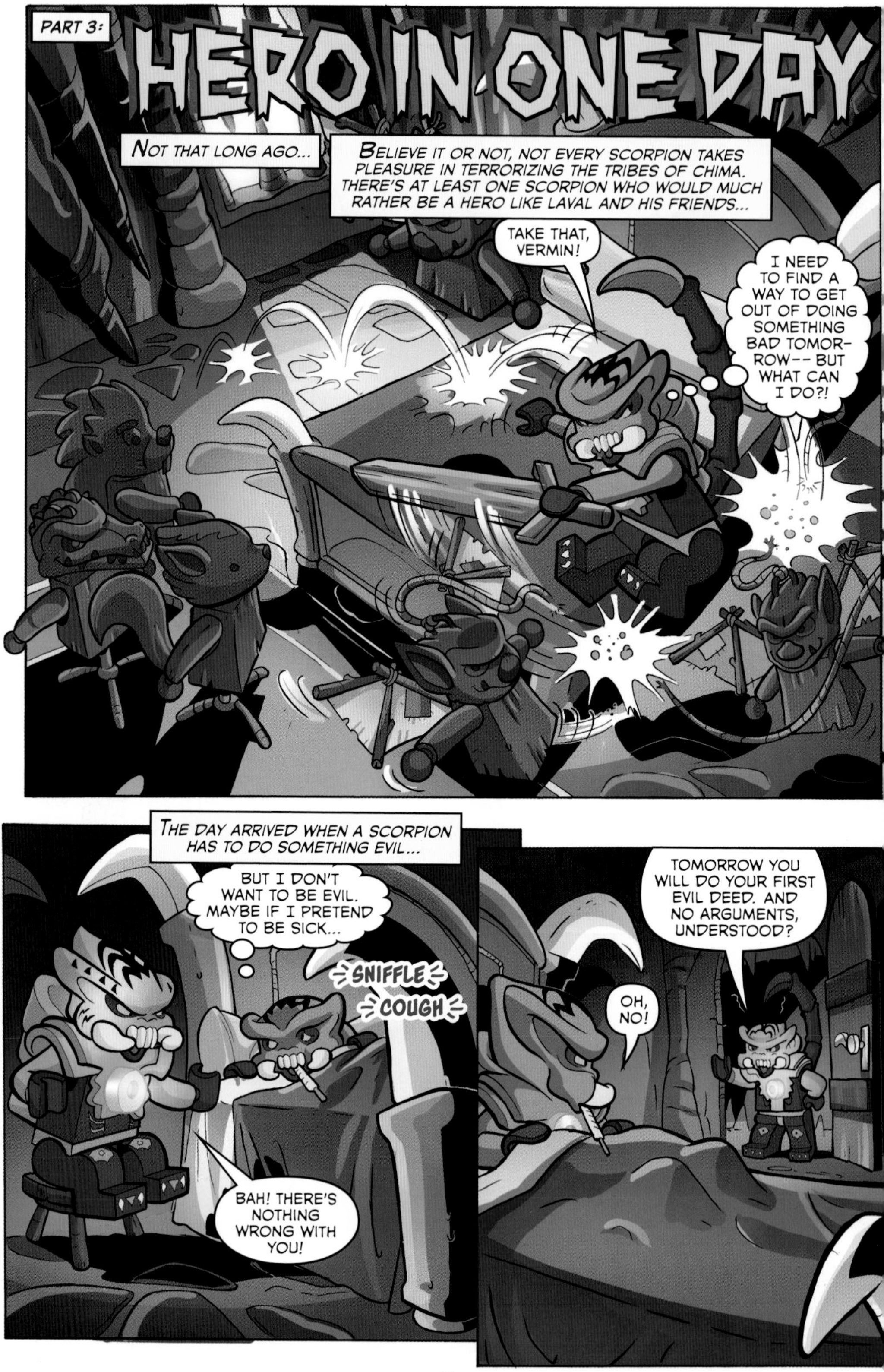
PART 3:
HERO IN ONE DAY
NOT THAT LONG AGO...
BELIEVE IT OR NOT, NOT EVERY SCORPION TAKES PLEASURE IN TERRORIZING THE TRIBES OF CHIMA. THERE'S AT LEAST ONE SCORPION WHO WOULD MUCH RATHER BE A HERO LIKE LAVAL AND HIS FRIENDS...
TAKE THAT, VERMIN!
I NEED TO FIND A WAY TO GET OUT OF DOING SOMETHING BAD TOMOR-ROW-- BUT WHAT CAN I DO?!
THE DAY ARRIVED WHEN A SCORPION HAS TO DO SOMETHING EVIL...
BUT I DON'T WANT TO BE EVIL. MAYBE IF I PRETEND TO BE SICK...
SNIFFLE
COUGH
BAH! THERE'S NOTHING WRONG WITH YOU!
TOMORROW YOU WILL DO YOUR FIRST EVIL DEED. AND NO ARGUMENTS, UNDERSTOOD?
OH, NO!

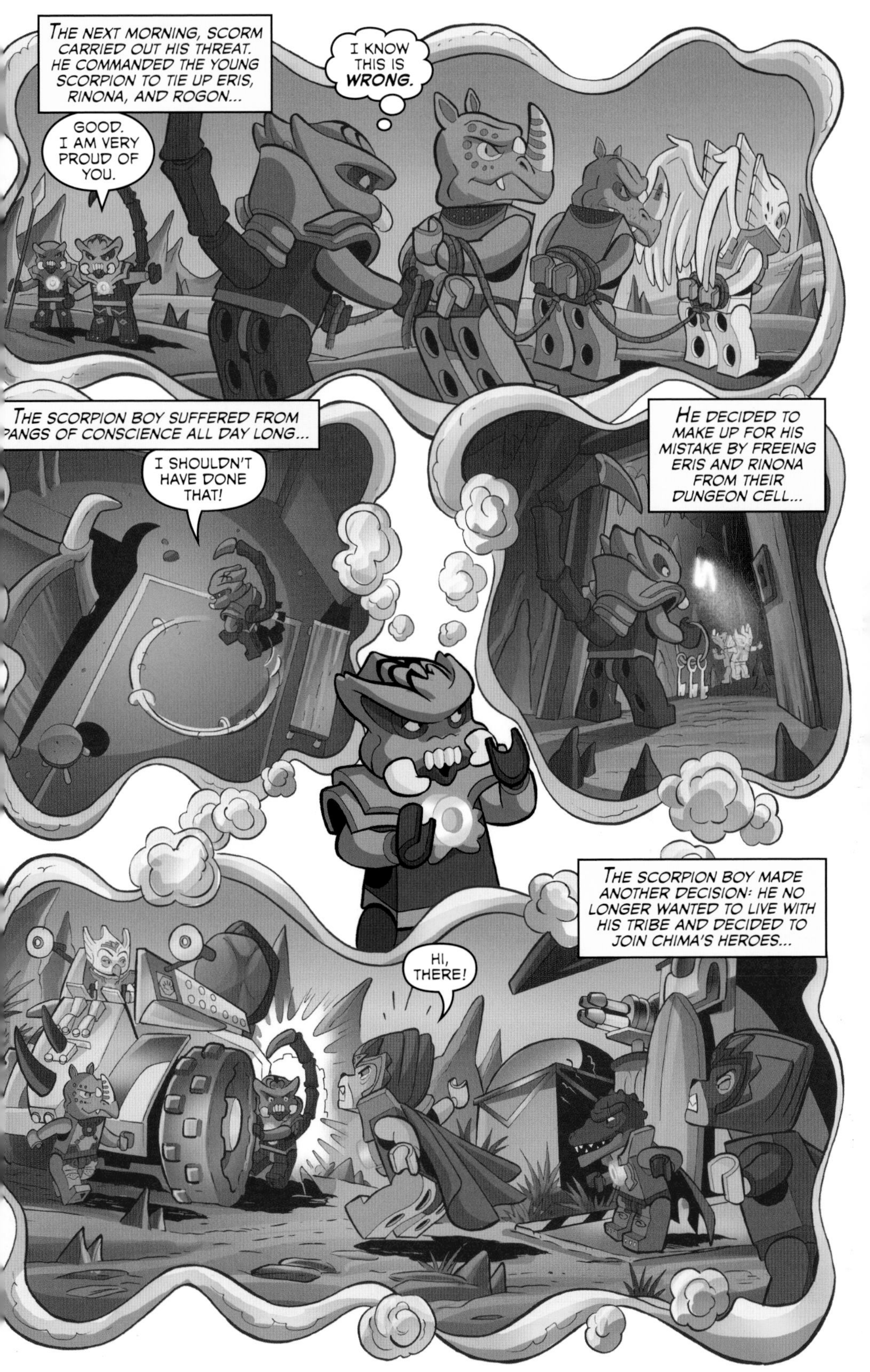
THE NEXT MORNING, SCORM CARRIED OUT HIS THREAT. HE COMMANDED THE YOUNG SCORPION TO TIE UP ERIS, RINONA, AND ROGON...
I KNOW THIS IS WRONG.
GOOD. I AM VERY PROUD OF YOU.
THE SCORPION BOY SUFFERED FROM PANGS OF CONSCIENCE ALL DAY LONG...
I SHOULDN'T HAVE DONE THAT!
HE DECIDED TO MAKE UP FOR HIS MISTAKE BY FREEING ERIS AND RINONA FROM THEIR DUNGEON CELL...
THE SCORPION BOY MADE ANOTHER DECISION: HE NO LONGER WANTED TO LIVE WITH HIS TRIBE AND DECIDED TO JOIN CHIMA'S HEROES...
HI, THERE!

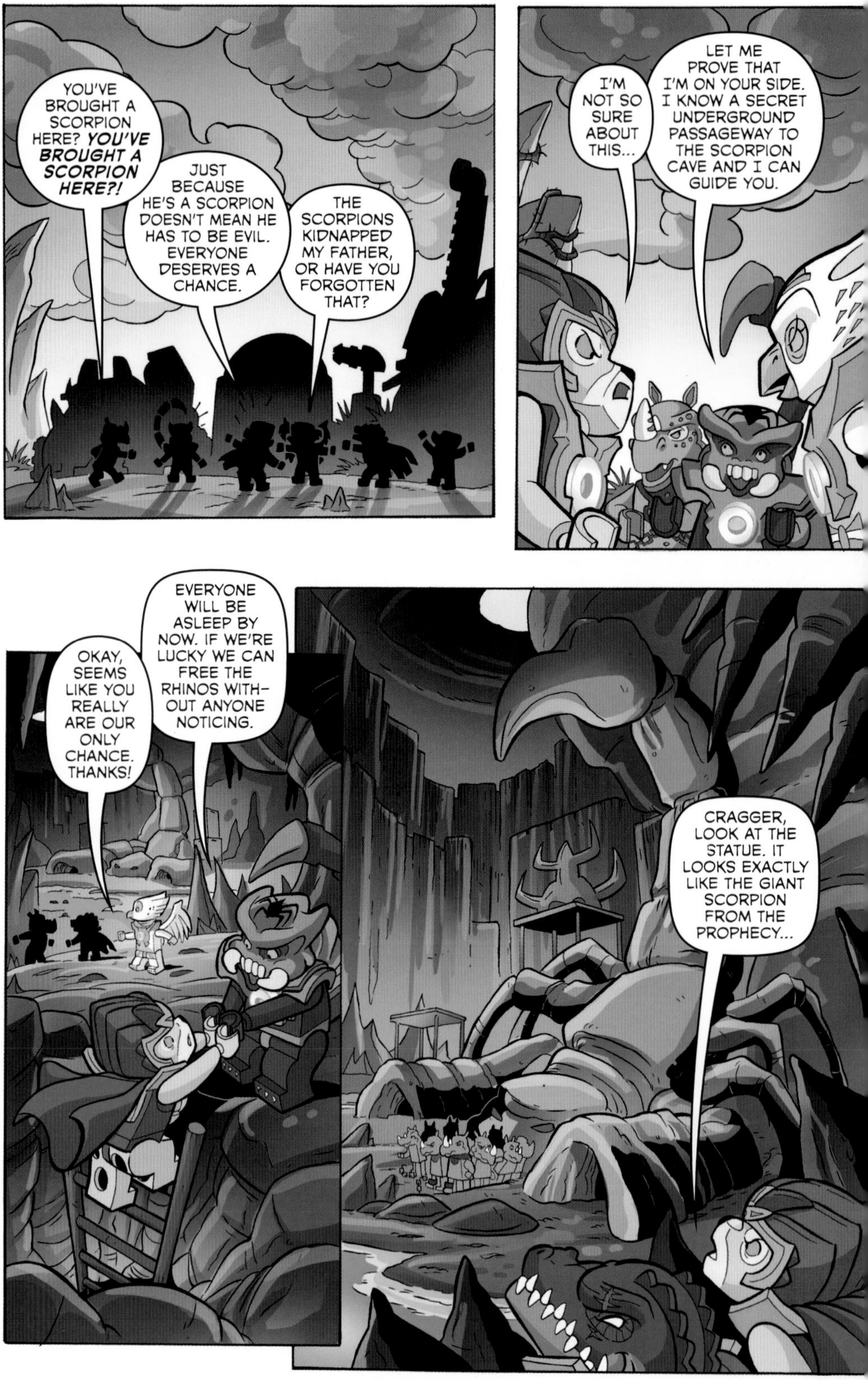
YOU'VE BROUGHT A SCORPION HERE? ***YOU'VE BROUGHT A SCORPION HERE?!***
JUST BECAUSE HE'S A SCORPION DOESN'T MEAN HE HAS TO BE EVIL. EVERYONE DESERVES A CHANCE.
THE SCORPIONS KIDNAPPED MY FATHER, OR HAVE YOU FORGOTTEN THAT?
I'M NOT SO SURE ABOUT THIS...
LET ME PROVE THAT I'M ON YOUR SIDE. I KNOW A SECRET UNDERGROUND PASSAGEWAY TO THE SCORPION CAVE AND I CAN GUIDE YOU.
OKAY, SEEMS LIKE YOU REALLY ARE OUR ONLY CHANCE. THANKS!
EVERYONE WILL BE ASLEEP BY NOW. IF WE'RE LUCKY WE CAN FREE THE RHINOS WITH-OUT ANYONE NOTICING.
CRAGGER, LOOK AT THE STATUE. IT LOOKS EXACTLY LIKE THE GIANT SCORPION FROM THE PROPHECY...

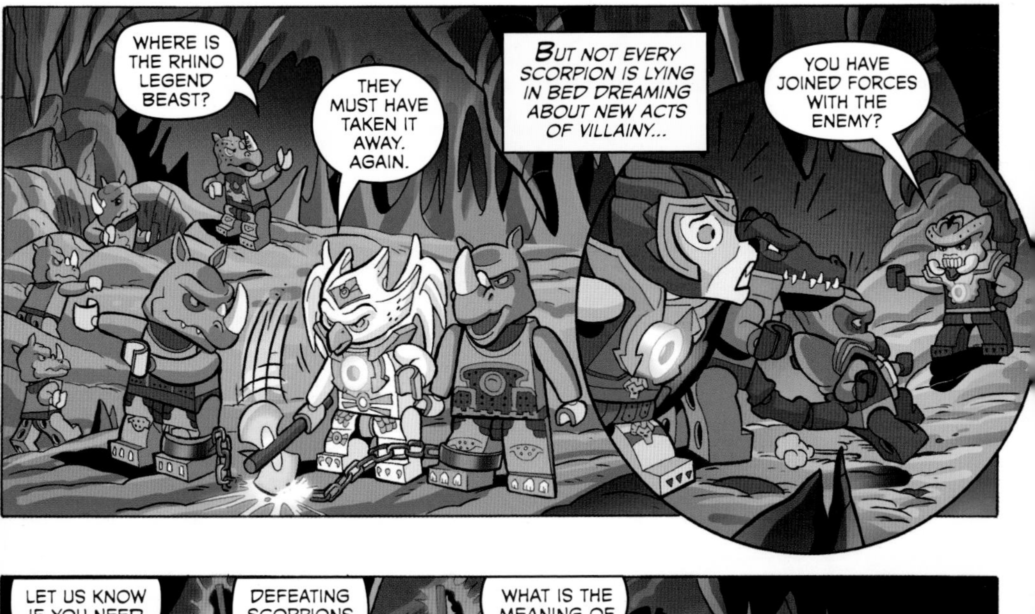
WHERE IS THE RHINO LEGEND BEAST?
THEY MUST HAVE TAKEN IT AWAY. AGAIN.
BUT NOT EVERY SCORPION IS LYING IN BED DREAMING ABOUT NEW ACTS OF VILLAINY...
YOU HAVE JOINED FORCES WITH THE ENEMY?

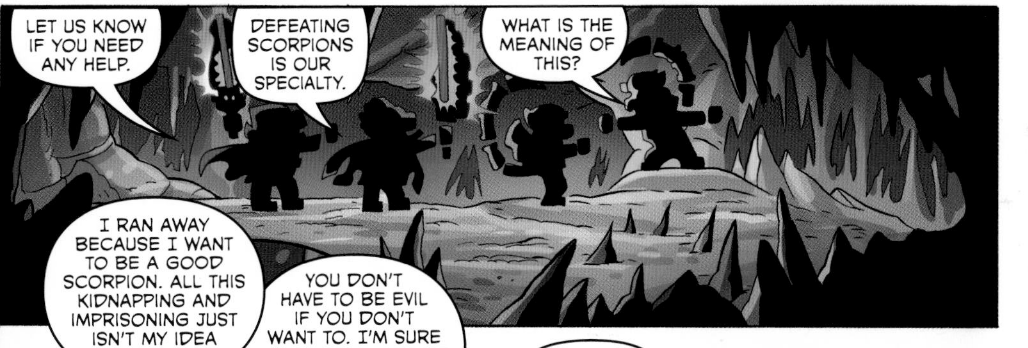
LET US KNOW IF YOU NEED ANY HELP.
DEFEATING SCORPIONS IS OUR SPECIALTY.
WHAT IS THE MEANING OF THIS?

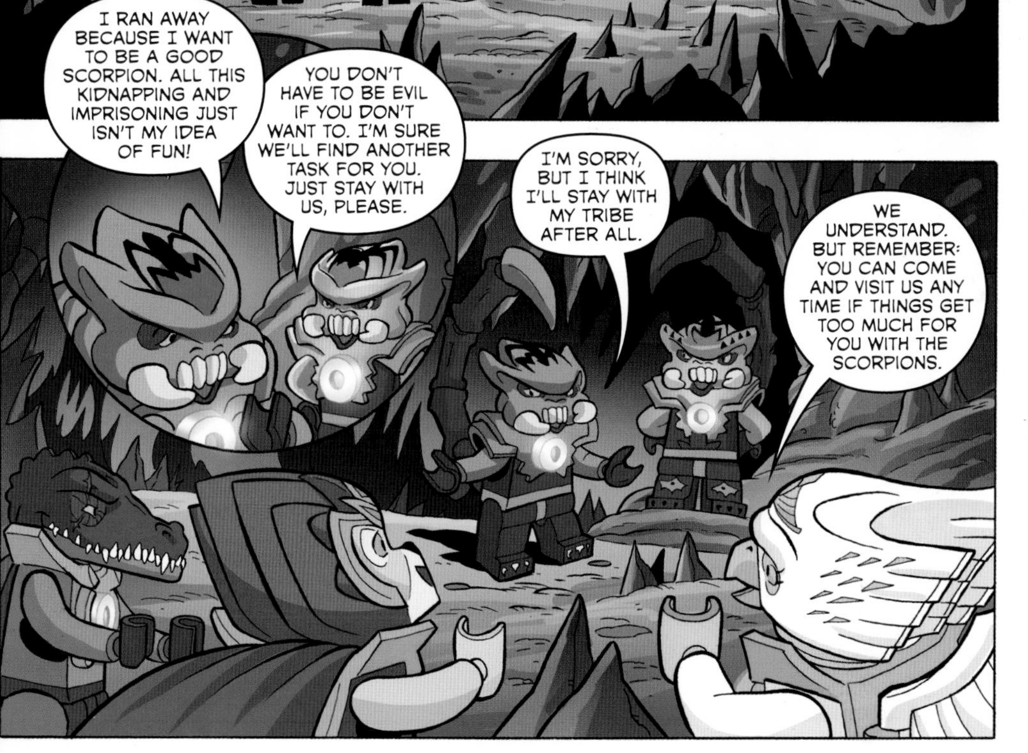
I RAN AWAY BECAUSE I WANT TO BE A GOOD SCORPION. ALL THIS KIDNAPPING AND IMPRISONING JUST ISN'T MY IDEA OF FUN!
YOU DON'T HAVE TO BE EVIL IF YOU DON'T WANT TO. I'M SURE WE'LL FIND ANOTHER TASK FOR YOU. JUST STAY WITH US, PLEASE.
I'M SORRY, BUT I THINK I'LL STAY WITH MY TRIBE AFTER ALL.
WE UNDERSTAND. BUT REMEMBER: YOU CAN COME AND VISIT US ANY TIME IF THINGS GET TOO MUCH FOR YOU WITH THE SCORPIONS.

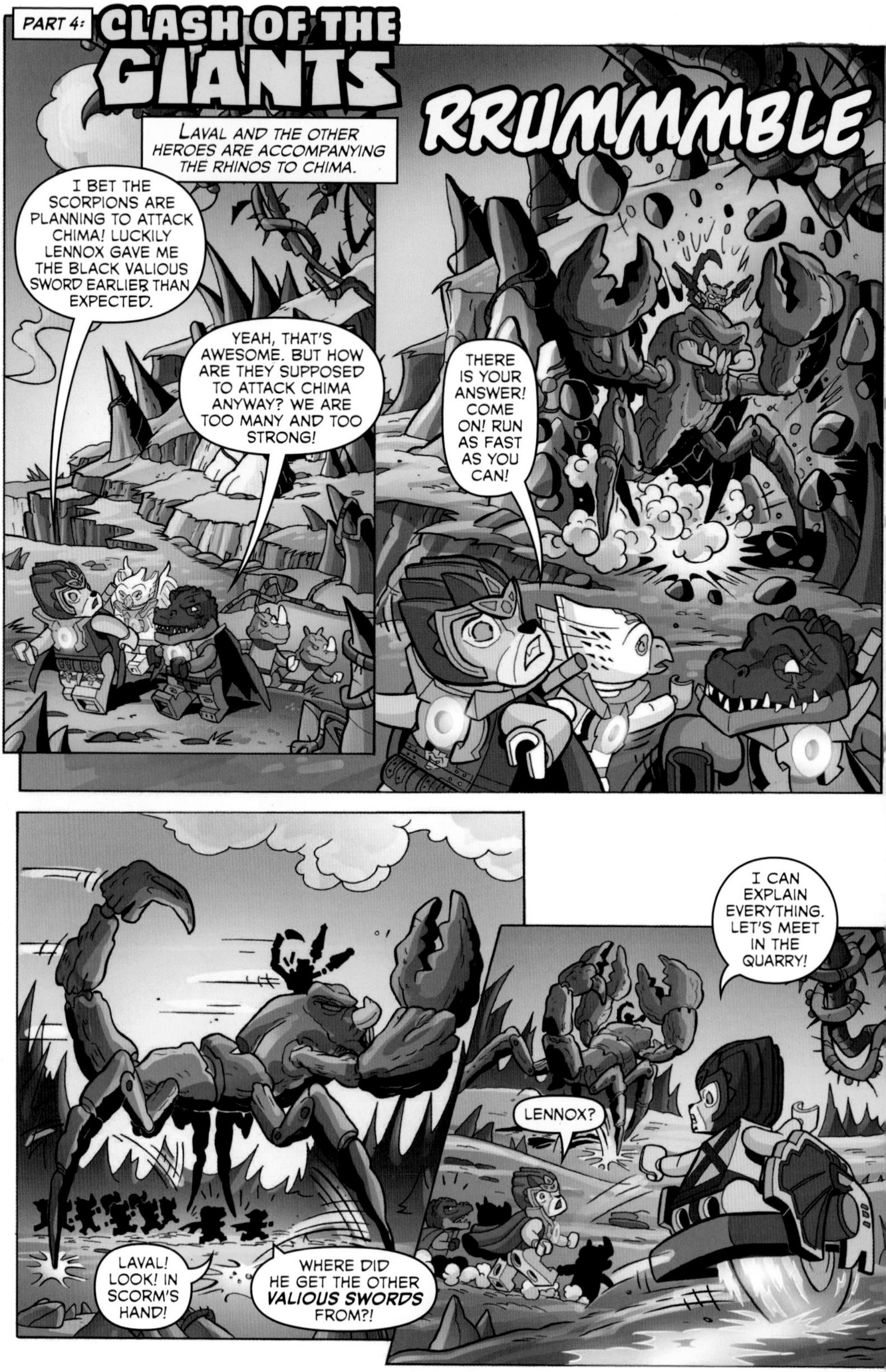
PART 4: CLASH OF THE GIANTS
LAVAL AND THE OTHER HEROES ARE ACCOMPANYING THE RHINOS TO CHIMA.
I BET THE SCORPIONS ARE PLANNING TO ATTACK CHIMA! LUCKILY LENNOX GAVE ME THE BLACK VALIOUS SWORD EARLIER THAN EXPECTED.
YEAH, THAT'S AWESOME. BUT HOW ARE THEY SUPPOSED TO ATTACK CHIMA ANYWAY? WE ARE TOO MANY AND TOO STRONG!
RRUMMMBLE
THERE IS YOUR ANSWER! COME ON! RUN AS FAST AS YOU CAN!
LAVAL! LOOK! IN SCORM'S HAND!
WHERE DID HE GET THE OTHER VALIOUS SWORDS FROM?!
LENNOX?
I CAN EXPLAIN EVERYTHING. LET'S MEET IN THE QUARRY!

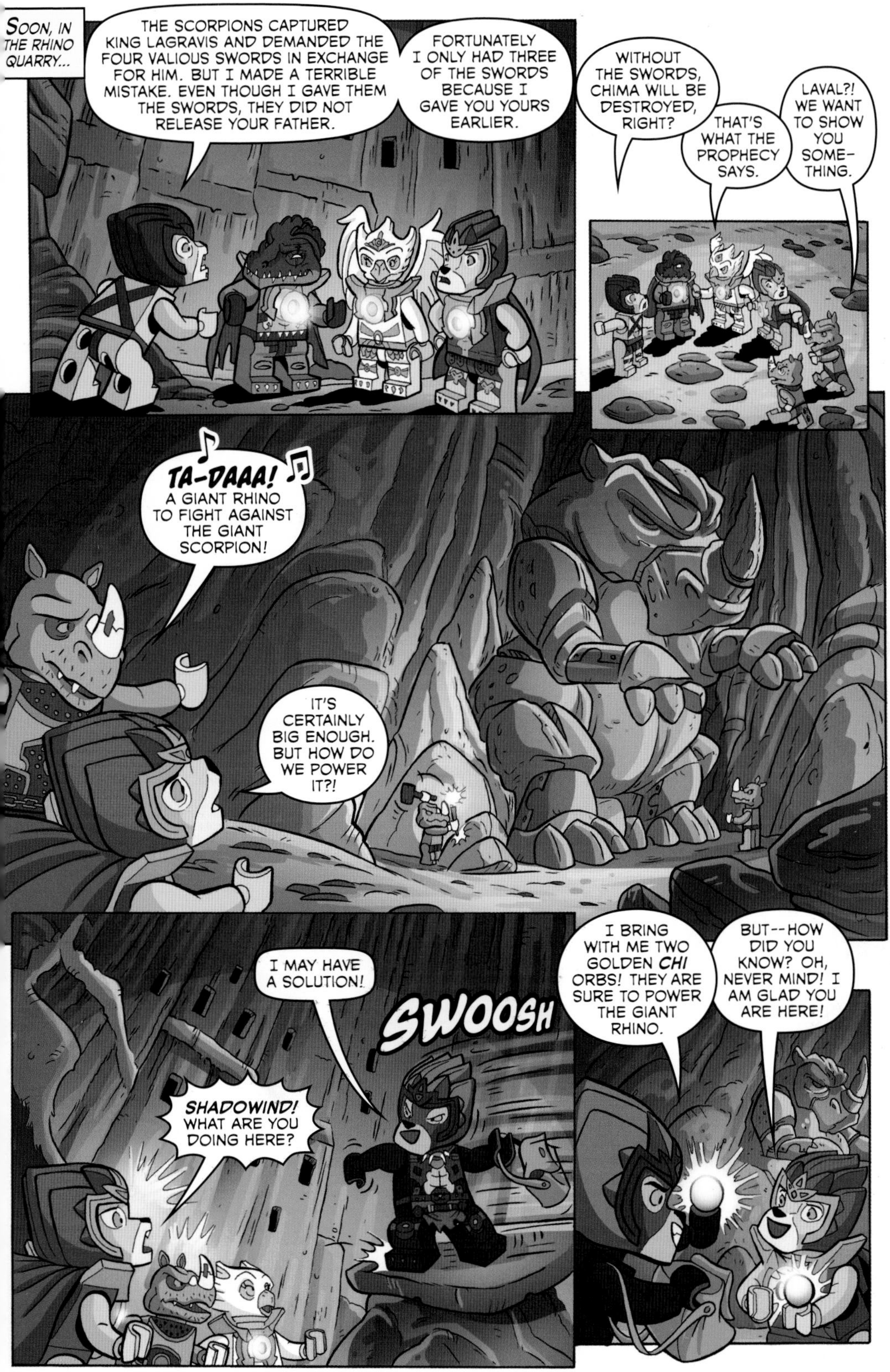
SOON, IN THE RHINO QUARRY...
THE SCORPIONS CAPTURED KING LAGRAVIS AND DEMANDED THE FOUR VALIOUS SWORDS IN EXCHANGE FOR HIM. BUT I MADE A TERRIBLE MISTAKE. EVEN THOUGH I GAVE THEM THE SWORDS, THEY DID NOT RELEASE YOUR FATHER.
FORTUNATELY I ONLY HAD THREE OF THE SWORDS BECAUSE I GAVE YOU YOURS EARLIER.
WITHOUT THE SWORDS, CHIMA WILL BE DESTROYED, RIGHT?
THAT'S WHAT THE PROPHECY SAYS.
LAVAL?! WE WANT TO SHOW YOU SOME-THING.
TA-DAAA! A GIANT RHINO TO FIGHT AGAINST THE GIANT SCORPION!
IT'S CERTAINLY BIG ENOUGH. BUT HOW DO WE POWER IT?!
I MAY HAVE A SOLUTION!
SWOOSH
SHADOWIND! WHAT ARE YOU DOING HERE?
I BRING WITH ME TWO GOLDEN CHI ORBS! THEY ARE SURE TO POWER THE GIANT RHINO.
BUT--HOW DID YOU KNOW? OH, NEVER MIND! I AM GLAD YOU ARE HERE!

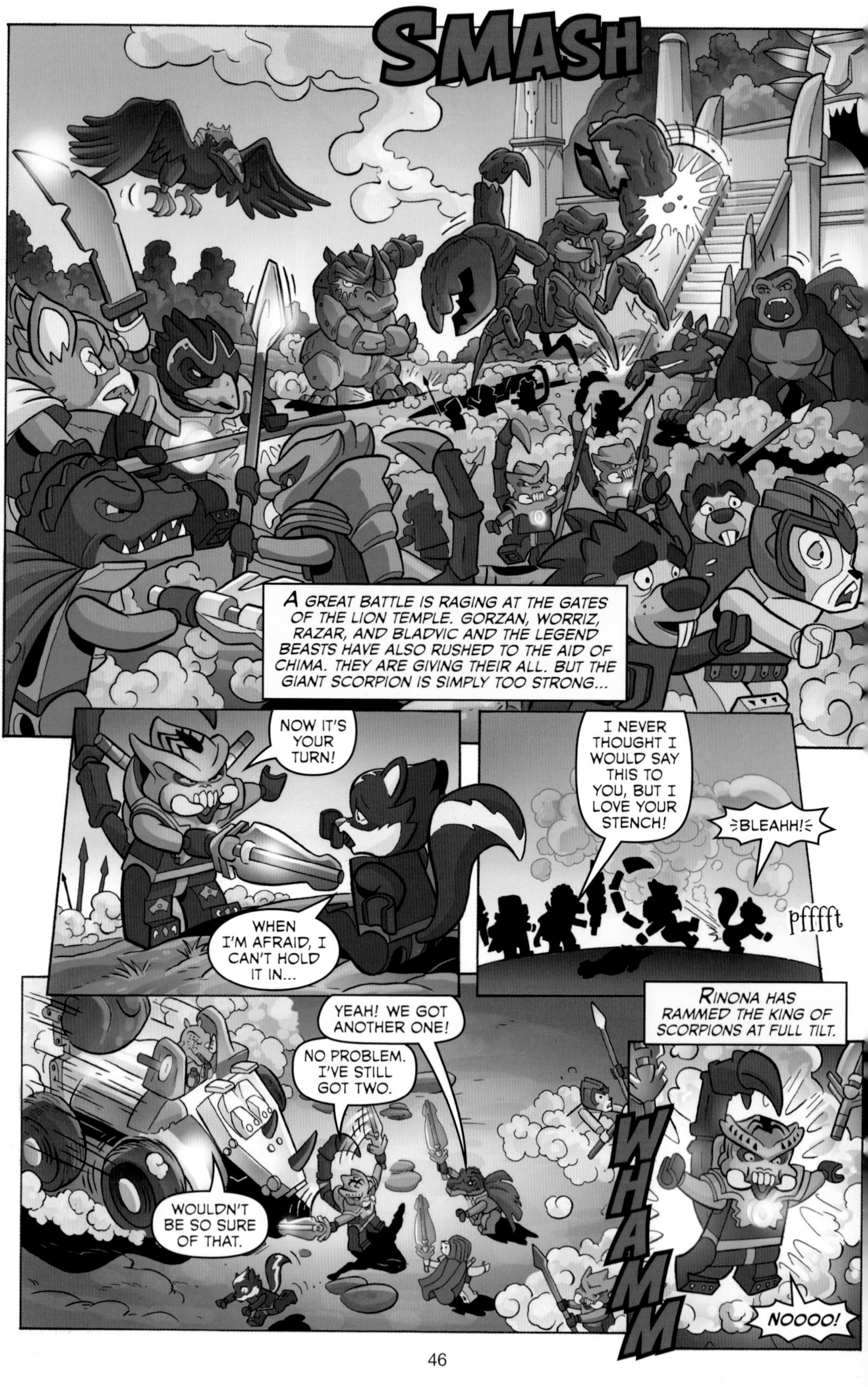
SMASH
A GREAT BATTLE IS RAGING AT THE GATES OF THE LION TEMPLE. GORZAN, WORRIZ, RAZAR, AND BLADVIC AND THE LEGEND BEASTS HAVE ALSO RUSHED TO THE AID OF CHIMA. THEY ARE GIVING THEIR ALL. BUT THE GIANT SCORPION IS SIMPLY TOO STRONG...
NOW IT'S YOUR TURN!
WHEN I'M AFRAID, I CAN'T HOLD IT IN...
I NEVER THOUGHT I WOULD SAY THIS TO YOU, BUT I LOVE YOUR STENCH!
BLEAHH!
pfffft
RINONA HAS RAMMED THE KING OF SCORPIONS AT FULL TILT.
YEAH! WE GOT ANOTHER ONE!
NO PROBLEM. I'VE STILL GOT TWO.
WOULDN'T BE SO SURE OF THAT.
WHAMM
NOOOO!

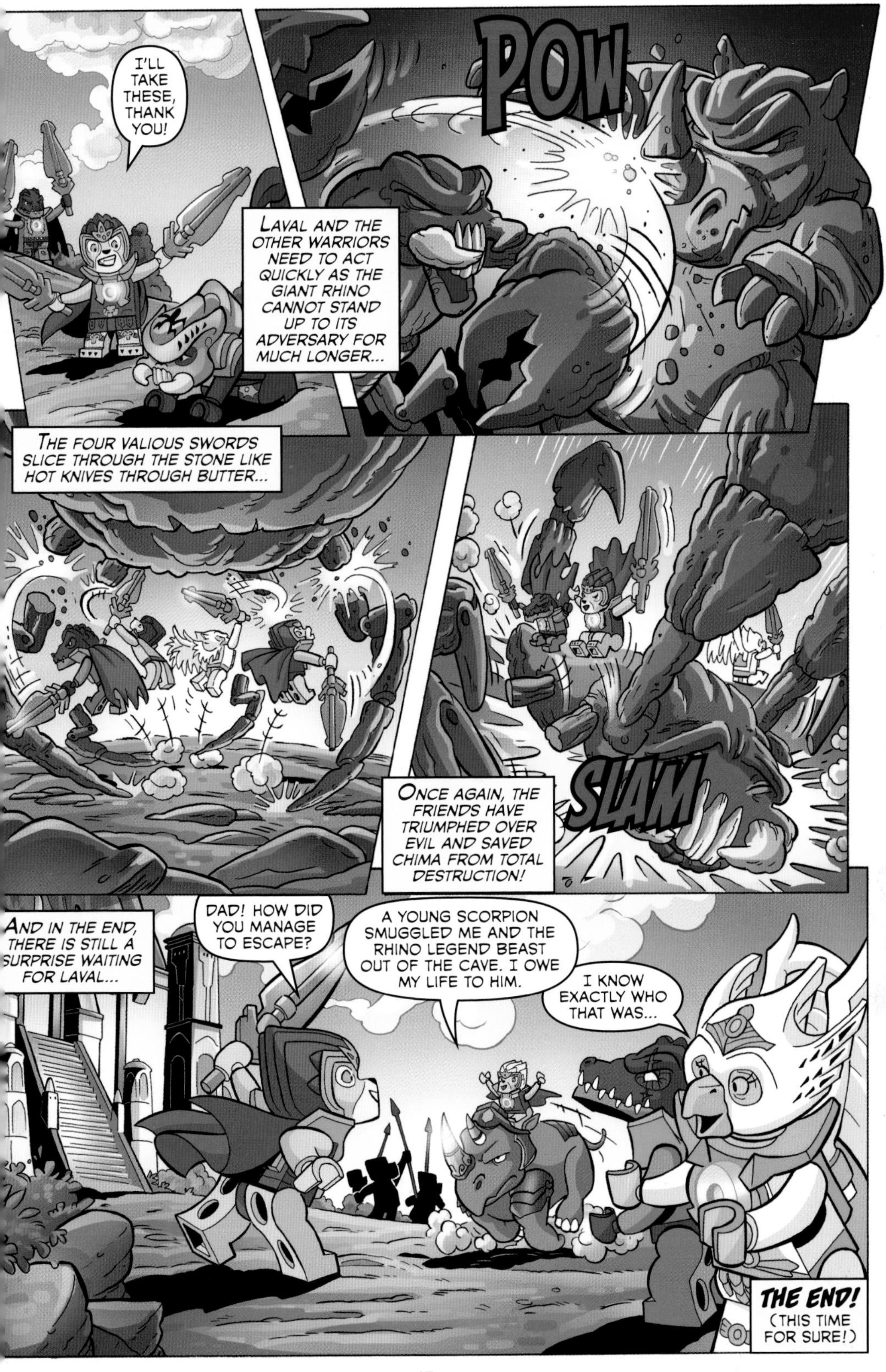
I'LL TAKE THESE, THANK YOU!
POW
LAVAL AND THE OTHER WARRIORS NEED TO ACT QUICKLY AS THE GIANT RHINO CANNOT STAND UP TO ITS ADVERSARY FOR MUCH LONGER...
THE FOUR VALIOUS SWORDS SLICE THROUGH THE STONE LIKE HOT KNIVES THROUGH BUTTER...
SLAM
ONCE AGAIN, THE FRIENDS HAVE TRIUMPHED OVER EVIL AND SAVED CHIMA FROM TOTAL DESTRUCTION!
AND IN THE END, THERE IS STILL A SURPRISE WAITING FOR LAVAL...
DAD! HOW DID YOU MANAGE TO ESCAPE?
A YOUNG SCORPION SMUGGLED ME AND THE RHINO LEGEND BEAST OUT OF THE CAVE. I OWE MY LIFE TO HIM.
I KNOW EXACTLY WHO THAT WAS...
THE END!
(THIS TIME FOR SURE!)